To my DEAR Sister

limes. Amen.

[signature]

29th MAY 2011

A Woman's Secret

A Story of Life, Love & Tragedy

Toyin Adon-Abel

authorHOUSE

AuthorHouse™
1663 Liberty Drive
Bloomington, IN 47403
www.authorhouse.com
Phone: 1-800-839-8640

© 2009 Toyin Adon-Abel. All rights reserved.

No part of this book may be reproduced, stored in a retrieval system, or transmitted by any means without the written permission of the author.

First published by AuthorHouse   11/29/2009

ISBN: 978-1-4490-2519-9 (e)
ISBN: 978-1-4490-2520-5 (sc)
ISBN: 978-1-4490-2521-2 (hc)

Library of Congress Control Number: 2009909206

Printed in the United States of America
Bloomington, Indiana

This book is printed on acid-free paper.

A Woman's Secret is a work of fiction, all names, places and incidents are figments of the author's imagination or have been used fictitiously. Any semblance to any person/s living or deceased is purely coincidental.

Toyin_book1@yahoo.com

ACKNOWLEDGEMENTS

I take this opportunity to first and foremost thank Almighty God for His blessings, without which, I would be nothing. His grace, His mercies, and His love keep me going always and they endure forever.

I spent nearly 6 years writing this novel and that is not including a previous number of years of research into the subject matter. As interested and gung-ho as I was in finishing the book, I had to deal with what for me was a major negative aspect… typing! I wrote 'A Woman's Secret' in long hand, which was absolutely fine by me. However, the idea and practise of transcribing the manuscript… punching the computer keyboard for hours on end practically drove me round the bend. And as such I thank both my beautiful wife Abi and my son Toyin (jnr.) for their patience and their typing skills. If not for them I might *still* be picking away at the keys till the next millennium!

Tomi, my lovely daughter…you read my book, thank you for your encouragement.

Dara, my lovely baby daughter…thank you for your wise suggestions.

Kiitan, my baby son…I can not wish for greater inspiration!

To Mum; Aotola…your love and support have always been unwavering.

I also thank Dr. Funmi Dairo, Dr. Folake Taylor, Dr. Bunmi Obayomi, Dr. Myra Herbert and especially my brother Dr. (Pastor) Albert Odulele. Without their medical knowledge and experiences I would have been totally lost in a world of medical science, genetics and internal medicine. Not to even mention the terminology, this at times almost convinced me to take a course in Latin.

Finally, I would like to extend my heartfelt gratitude to all my dear friends and relatives who not only encouraged me but have also patiently and sometimes *impatiently* waited for me to not only complete this book, but to start on its sequel and all the other books I have within me. Thank you!

My prayer for everyone I have mentioned here and for all I may have unwittingly overlooked is… May the Lord God Almighty continue to bless and favour you in everything you lay your hands upon to do. Amen.

For my father; Abel…may your soul rest in everlasting peace. Amen

PROLOGUE
SYDNEY COLLINS-CALDWELL

April.
Salou, Spain.

In all things and at all times I remain thankful. After all, both I and my baby are healthy. I just wish that my husband had felt the same way! I am the master of my fate, the captain of my soul, at least that's what I had been told over and over again as I grew up. Mama had constantly said that I could become whatsoever I chose. Now as an adult I realize that I can control my destiny only up to a certain point. What I have experienced in my personal life recently is not what I would have scripted for myself.

As I walk along the beach, I feel the white sand between my toes and under my bare feet. I look up at the setting sun and the orange and blue evening sky and I wonder at God's creations. The sea waves lapping upon one another, the slight breeze, the fresh air, even the little red crabs I see scuttling around but mostly I look into the little face of my baby girl Teri in my arms. My relationship with her is unusual to say the least. In the years to come I have to decide exactly how to tell her about her heritage and pray that it does not affect her adversely. Maybe I shouldn't tell her at all! The confusion and the questions are still looming large in my mind; I don't even know what will be best for either of us.

I begin to feel better after my walk; I take in a deep breath, savoring the scent of the sea and the sand, remembering why I love this part of the world so much.

A sudden gust of wind pulls at the woolen blanket around Teri and I hold her closer. It seems that the temperature has dropped. I decide that I've been outside long enough and start back toward my hotel. I think about how my life has changed dramatically over just 3 years. I have gone from a rich kid, graduate of an Ivy League college, to married woman, to mother. College was great, being married to Linc had been super great and being a mother is the most fulfilling experience I've ever had. Countless times in her 3 months of life, I have gently pulled on Teri's toes and fingers, caressed her face, her hair and kissed her. To me she's a tiny angel and despite the circumstances of her birth she'll always be special. I arrive back at the hotel and feed and bathe her. After she had fallen asleep I settle in for another possible sleepless night and once again pine for my husband. I grab a carrot from my half-eaten salad take a bite and put it back down. I decide to call somebody. Who should I call? Dad, Carla? …. Definitely not Mama though! I'm not sure. I ponder for a moment, pick up the phone and begin to dial.

CHAPTER 1
SYDNEY COLLINS

Wednesday April 11th
Boston, MA
3 years earlier.

I toss and turn in my bed; I can feel the sunlight streaming through my yellow Venetian blinds onto my pillow.

"Hmmm seems like it's going to be a wonderful day" I murmur sleepily.

I must have drifted off because all of a sudden I am back in my dream. I'm a caterpillar forming a cocoon. While the cocoon forms a voice tells me that I need to decide what color and size I'm going to be as a butterfly and asks where am I going to live.

"It doesn't matter. I've been waiting for this day all my life; do you think I ever stop to think about those minor details?" I say in the dream.

I continue swaying back and forth while my cocoon forms. I remember it being a feeling of both joy and anticipation.

Suddenly, the swaying becomes very violent and I feel smothered, I try to take a full breath but can't. I open my eyes just as I could feel and smell someone pressing down on me. This *can't* be Omar again can it? The last time he did something like this I'd nearly made him a eunuch! I start struggling, kicking out my legs and trying to get up while at the same time trying to scream. But I can't, the person's hand over my mouth is too strong. I continue to struggle, trying to bite any part of the person's body I can reach.

I feel a hand on my breast; I intensify my struggling digging my nails into the unwelcome hand.

We roll off the bed landing in a heap on the carpet. I suddenly recognize the person's smell as I see him.

"Omar! What the heck do you think you're doing?" I shout, enraged.

"How did you get into my bedroom?" I scream, jumping up from the floor and trying to adjust my night shirt.

"Omar! Answer me you idiot."

"What the heck is wrong with you? I warned you last time that I'll call the cops and have you arrested"

I lunge at him, swinging both arms, trying to scratch his eyes out. But he grabs my arms as I continue to struggle as hard as I can. I free one arm and slap him across the face as hard as I can.

"Are you crazy?"

I continue kicking and punching him. I'm as angry as I've ever been and his silence isn't helping the situation any.

"You *are* crazy Omar; you want me to call out to Dad?"

"Pops? He ain't home, I saw him drive off just as I got here" he finally says.

"I don't give a damn" I respond, just as I'm able to connect with a kick to his groin.

"Oomph, damn it Sidney, did you really have to do that?"

"Get out! Get out of my room!"

I'm screaming at him now and pushing him, propelling him toward the door. In his doubled up position he bangs his head on the door frame and angrily elbows me in the stomach.

"Aah! negro you hit me"

He finally escapes from the room just as the heavy candle I throw at him shatters on the edge of the door, narrowly missing his already banged up head.

This time Omar has gone too far! I'm tired of him following me around like a puppy dog and now he's sneaked into my bedroom again and assaulted me. He's just a friend and although he can be very nice and helpful at times enough is enough! I must have told him a million times that ain't nothing gonna happen. Angrily I walk into my bathroom.

"I need to go straighten that negro out" I say out loud to myself.

"And I will be calling the cops"

I brush my teeth and step into the shower; I'm still seething mad at Omar.

"That boy is gonna make me knock out his teeth one of these days. I haven't so much as even kissed him before. Shucks!" I mumble.

A couple of club dates, one of those in a group with four other friends and this fool thinks he can now touch me?

"Heck no!"

I take time to relax a little under the warm water, scrubbing my favorite shower gel into my skin, my eyes closed. I remember that I still need to go see Dad at his office downtown, maybe I'll even tell Dad about that idiot Omar.

As I step out of the shower I also remember that last night Dad had insisted I go straight back to college and do a Master's degree. I've been accepted to all 3 graduate schools I applied to but I think I want to hold off on more studying for a while. Maybe Dad will let me go to New York and work for him. It shouldn't be too difficult to convince him, I'm his only child and I usually get what I want!

"Heck!" I've stubbed my pinkie toe on the corner of my dresser again. It's gotta be the 100th darn time. I've got to move it a few inches. Still muttering under my breath because of the pain in my toe, I apply my make up.

I throw on a white and blue checkered shirt, a pair of blue jeans and black heeled shoes. I grab my black fur lined leather jacket and storm out my bedroom, I'm still mad at Omar.

I run down the stairs to the den where I know Omar will be waiting. He'll either be watching Dad's recordings of CSI or eating Mama's cooking from dinner last night.

I see him taking a large bite out of a chicken leg. He looks up and grins as he hears me walk in.

"What the heck are you grinning at fool? I'm calling the cops, right now"

"Hold up, hold up Syd. You're not still mad at me are you?" He asks in a panic.

"I sure am; are you kidding me? I told you last time you pulled this stupid stunt. Didn't I?" I reply angrily.

"Come on Sydney, calm down baby. You know me just playing witya. No need to bring dem coppers here, ya know."

"Don't *baby* me negro, and don't try to make me smile with your fake Jamaican accent." I yell.

I walk right up to him, grab the plate of chicken, greens, corn, mashed potatoes and gravy he is eating and throw it all over his chest. And for good measure I throw his drink of apple juice into his face.

"How do you like that fool? I'm out to see Dad, clean up the mess behind you. You better not get Jones to do it either, *YOU* do it yourself." I say smirking.

And with that said I saunter out of the house to my car.

"Good! At least he won't be able to jump into my car with me." I murmur to myself.

"Hopefully I won't see him for the rest of the day. I'd better call Jones myself and instruct him not to clean up Omar's mess." I thought.

Jones is sort of like our maid or butler and knowing him he'll try to tidy things up himself.

I dial home from my cell.

"Good morning Jones. Sorry I had to rush out the house but I'm on my way to see Dad. Listen, Omar's made a mess in the den; I don't want you to clean it alright?"

"G'morn to you too Miss. Sydney, you know I can't let Mr. Omar……" he replies, before I cut him short.

"Jones! You must not do it okay? I'm very serious, do you hear me Jones?"

"Yes Ma'am" he responds

"Thanks Jones and sorry for cutting you short just now, bye." I hang up the phone and start my car.

It'll take me about 30 minutes to get to Dad's office downtown.

My Dad, Mr. Jordan Paul Collins is CEO of CSD (Computer Systems and Development) a very successful computer firm here in Boston. He also has offices in Atlanta GA, Fort Lauderdale, FL and Chicago, IL. It took me years to break through the "rich girl" stereotype that people tend to attach to me. In my opinion I'm not spoiled. Dad always stresses the value of hard work and education. He had urged me to take various internships throughout college before he would even give me the car I wanted. He always told me that if my grades dropped, so would my allowance. So basically I haven't been fed with a platinum spoon like most people would believe. Mama is pretty laid back. She and Dad have been married for a million years it seems. Mama doesn't have a career anymore but is actively involved in various non-profit organizations and is well respected throughout the community. The problem however is that neither gives me much credit when it comes to what I'm capable of accomplishing on my own.

"All that's about to change!" I say out loud. Loud enough for me to hear myself over the booming car stereo.

I have it all planned out. I'll invite him to brunch and I'll tell him straight out,

"Dad, I'm not going to grad school right now, I need some time to figure out what I really want and I need you to be supportive of my decision."

Then I'll stare him straight in the eyes and wait for his response. Is this plan really going to work? Well, there's only one way to find out....

I probably have just enough time to enter this building, ride the elevator to the 20th floor and walk into Dad's office before he leaves for his meeting. I had called him en-route and he'd told me about an impromptu meeting he has to attend. Here I am, in downtown Boston looking at the old rustic buildings side by side with modern ones. I've always loved this city, full of history and intrigue and money. Yes, money! There's nothing wrong with liking money and the privileges it can bring, privileges that can span one's immediate family and also a multitude of others. Others that one chooses to assist in one form or the other. I have always believed in my heart that wealth is meant to be shared. One of the reasons I love Dad so much and get along with him so well, is that he agrees with me. Dad *also* believes that he should help anyone less fortunate than us. Mama on the other hand! That's another story. She is the youngest child of a struggling family in Georgia and has let personal ambition get the better of her generous side. As a matter of fact, I can't remember her ever having a generous side. Whatever financial gain that comes Mama's way, stays with her further swelling her already swollen bank accounts. Mama has a very successful law firm that she moved from Atlanta to Boston within a year of marrying Dad. She doesn't practice regularly any longer but she spends almost all her time involved in charity work, not for the love of it, but to socialize with all the other multi-millionaire wives that participate in these events. Dad, I must admit relishes the fact that his beautiful, intelligent and successful wife, has the time to look after him to his heart's content. Who could blame him anyway? I can't. After all aren't love and contentment the most important elements of a lasting marriage? Sugar! Time to concentrate on my imminent meeting with Dad.

"Hello Jill" I say, strolling past his secretary in the outer office.

"Hi Sydney, how are you today?" she replies, as polite as ever.

I swing open the double wooden doors leading to his large office and I'm almost knocked off my feet as he picks me up in a bear hug, swings me around and kisses me on my forehead. As always Dad has a wide beaming smile, bearing all his very white teeth when he sees me. He makes me feel warm inside and constantly validates me.

"Sweetheart" he booms, "You are right on time, punctual as usual and pretty as ever!"

"Where are we having this brunch you've invited me to?" he continues, getting straight to the point in his typical fashion.

"It's almost 11am and I'm ready to eat "

"Slow down Dad" I say.

"I've decided we'll talk right here in your office, this way I'll try to be as straight to the point as you always are and not have to worry about any distractions. Could you instruct Jill that you don't want to be disturbed for the next half hour?"

Dad looks at me in silence for a few moments and then says

"Wow, this must be important. I see you really mean business. Let's go and sit over by the windows. If I can't eat I'll at least enjoy the panoramic view, the weather is lovely today."

"Thanks Dad" I respond,

"And try not to think of food too" I continue with a grin.

"You cheeky princess." Dad murmurs.

I sit down in the comfortable chair by the large Bay windows overlooking downtown Boston and the rest of the city. I then launch straight into my prepared little speech almost verbatim, even before he has completely settled into his armchair opposite me.

"Dad, I'm not going to grad school right now. I would like some time to figure out what I really want to do with my life and I need you to be supportive of my decision."

I take a deep sigh and wait for his response.

I'm sure it's been at least three minutes and Dad still hasn't said a word. Should I wait another three, or try to assert myself by saying something else. He's just staring at me confusingly, but do I detect a slight grin? I hope not. He's probably scheming

"Dad! Didn't you hear what I said? Aren't you going to say anything? What are you thinking? Why are you ignoring me? Are you angry? Say someth…"

"Slow down, take it easy sweetheart, you just worried me that's all. So what would you like to do?" Dad asks.

"Travel, work maybe?" I respond apprehensively.

"Fantastic! How would you like to oversee a new branch of CSD in New York? That would allow you to travel and work at the same time." He grins again.

This time *I* stare at him. I have a sneaky feeling that I've been set up. But how? He didn't know what I was coming to speak to him about. Does he know me that well? Dad clears his throat as if to speak, but I quickly interject.

"Dad, if I didn't know better, I'd say that you've had this planned all along."

"Actually, I have been considering Adam Whittaker out of the Ft. Lauderdale office for this assignment. But as you have just expressed your desire to travel and work, I trust you will do an excellent job. After all, you're a Summa Cum Laude graduate. In addition to that, you showed outstanding management skills during your internships." He concludes.

My mind is swirling, this seems like a lot of responsibility but it also sounds exciting. New York! *Wow*! What an opportunity this would be to see the Big Apple. I could cruise China town looking for art and décor, pop into as many cafés as I please and visit the splendid museums.

"Dad, does Mama know about this?"

"I haven't run this by her yet." He replies.

"Do you want to rush home and catch her before she jets off to Haiti?" He adds.

I wonder if I could make it home on time. Downtown to Beacon Hill where we live can take as long as 40 minutes at lunchtime.

"But Dad, you sure Mama's home? She wasn't when I left"

"Yeah baby princess, she is. She just called me from her room a couple of moments before you walked in here."

"Ok Dad, I'm heading straight home, I'll call Mama from my cell phone. Consider that I'm giving you a provisional thumb up to your proposal."

I get up excitedly, feeling as if a weight has been lifted off my mind. An executive in a multi-million dollar firm! I'll get a new car. The metallic blue Mercedes Benz SLK I have always wanted, a big office with one of those big black leather chairs and a large shiny plaque with my name on it. I'll even get my own secretary…hmm! A tall, dark, handsome firefighter I muse, laughing to myself.

"Behave yourself young lady," I tell myself, you're supposed to be renewing your mind.

I practically run out of Dad's office, barely pausing to say goodbye to Jill. I wait impatiently for the elevator; all I can think of is getting home to tell Mama before she leaves for the airport. I'm both excited and a little apprehensive about Dad's offer but I also know I just can't wait to get to New York.

Well, that went great after all. In fact, I really got the chance to challenge my own safety zone and it turned out well. As I scan my room to figure out what was going and what was definitely staying here, the phone rings.

"Hey who dat?" I ask.

"Hey Sydney, what's up? It's Omar."

"What do you want Omar?"

"Chill baby girl. I'm holding up a white flag and standing in the middle of my room in white boxers and socks, really!" He chuckles.

I can't help laughing out loud.

"You're so stupid Omar but I'm still mad at ya."

"Oh yeah!" He replies loudly.

"I haven't had this much free time since I was about 3 years old." We both giggle like kids.

"So," I ask.

"Are you still taking that job offer with IBM?"

"Yep." He responds in a tone that was all too familiar.

"Omar, what's the deal? You sound like you're not as excited about it as you were a month ago, when you got the offer. You punkin'out or what?"

"Nah" he replies nonchalantly,

"It's just that they're all serious and stuff-shirt you know. I mean I know I can't really be myself with those guys but the money is off the chain and *I am* kind of psyched to move out to L.A."

"Well then, there's no problem."

I want to sound as reassuring to him as Dad had sounded to me.

"You'll adjust fine. IBM needs a brother up in there that can keep it real and get the job done. They'll probably surprise you and be cooler than you think. Besides, with all the action going on in L.A. you can be stuff-shirt in the daytime and wild at night!"

He laughs and tells me that he is definitely going to try it out. He says he's worried about coming off like a sellout to his boys. That is such a cop out! His boys want the same success he has and from what I've seen, they are supportive. He just has the jitters; I know the symptoms all too well. We chit chat a bit more then agree to meet later for dinner. Omar is cool to chill with. I just need to keep re-enforcing it to him that we are just going to be friends. Maybe I should have called the cops on him earlier on. He had seemed scared at the time which is a good sign that he won't do it again.

While I'm actually in the mood to talk I call a couple of friends (I only had about four) and tell them about my decision. They are all cool with it and most of us planned on getting out of Boston anyway. Boston is great but we have all agreed that a change of pace, either through graduate studies or working would be a welcomed change. My girl Tiffany has got an offer that requires a three-month training program in Spain. Now that was a change of pace! I am in no rush to leave the country. I've done study programs abroad in Mexico and Kenya and I've enjoyed myself, but there's nothing like the comforts of the good 'ole U.S. of A. As I rummage through my belongings, I realize that there aren't many things that I'm attached to.

CHAPTER 2
RYOKO YOKOZUNA

Wednesday April 11th
Queens Village, NY

"I could sure do with a drink; even just water would be great." I whisper into my police mic.

"Damn it Ryoko, shut the hell up! Maintain radio silence…. you've been bitching about a drink for the past 30 minutes, like a rookie."

"Don't make me get out my van and wring your bull-like neck Sarge…" I retort

"You know I'd love to, don't tempt me." I continue, whispering.

"Man! Would one of ya'll out there get this woman to shut up." Sarge grunts back into his mic.

I really *do* feel like getting out of my van and karate chopping this idiot's neck. Sarge Goon we all call him, but his real name is Bill Lagoon, he gets on everyone's nerves with his grunts, loud farts and general obnoxious behavior. But he's right I'd better forget my thirst for now and concentrate on this stake out.

It's almost pitch black out here tonight. The only faint light is coming from a street light nearly 50 yards down the road, and its reflection off a couple of the parked cars. I look at my watch…9:46p.m. Gee, we've been out here for 3 hours already. There are 4 officers in total, all of us in plain clothes, sitting in 4 different vehicles. None of us look like a cop tonight; to varying degrees we all look like homeless people who've found some unlocked vehicles to sleep in. Each of our vehicles is parked about 35-40 yards apart, along the same street in lower end Queens. We've got our radios, handcuffs and guns hidden in our clothing. I pat my Glock 21 SF reassuringly. I adjust my position in my seat and smile ruefully. Patting my Glock again I feel very reassured, the gun's 13+1 capacity of .45 AUTO cartridges gives me great stopping power. More than enough to stop a 300lb, drug induced, perp! Because that's the prey tonight, plus I also got my Springfield XD9 subcompact strapped to my ankle as backup.

"Heads up Ryoko, you've got an unidentified coming up behind you real sharpish....!"

The warning from Sarge comes too late! Before I can even look in my rear view mirror or turn around I hear.

"Freeze bitch! Get out the van reeeeal slow; leave the keys right where they are. If you make one wrong move I'll blow your damn head off."

He jams his gun hard into the left side of my head, hard enough for me to feel the skin break and blood ooze out. I take a second before moving, trying to buy a little time, also giving my colleagues time to react.

"You deaf bitch?" the perp asks angrily, as he again jams his gun into my head.

This time I react instinctively.

I grab his gun hand with my right hand, jamming my finger into the trigger with his, causing the gun to go off three times. The sound of the shots right next to my ears in such close quarters, and the sound of the breaking windshield as the bullets smash through it, deafens me temporarily. In the distance for a second or two I can hear Sarge and the other officers on the radio running towards me.

I continue to struggle with the perp while trying to reach over my waist with my left hand, to pull out my Glock from my waist band.

"Shit…my gun has fallen to the floor of the car…damn it."

I'm sure he hears the clunk as it hit the floor.

He must have figured out what I'm trying to do too 'cos he then slams the butt of his gun into my jaw with both hands and fires again…

The sudden pain in my jaw is bad enough but it pales in comparison to the agony in my head. I feel a combined sensation of lightheadedness, agony and fury. My last thought as I pass out is….. this s………h isn't going kill me and get away with it!

I come round a few moments later to the concerned voices of Sarge and Officer Kent. There is blood all over my face, neck, shoulders and chest. I'm feeling dizzy and my head feels like it's been sliced open with a red hot scalpel.

I hear several shots being fired; I can recognize the sound of police 38specials and I also recollect the sound of the perp's gun as he returns fire.

"Get after him guys he's trying to make it to the abandoned warehouse at the end of the street. Cut him off, run him down don't let him get away." Sarge bellows.

Sarge and Kent gently pull me out of the van and lay me down on the pavement.

"You okay Ryoko?" Kent asks.

"The EMS is on its way, looks like a pretty bad flesh wound girl, but good thing is you'll live. *You must have more than 9 fricking lives*! Damn it Ryoko why didn't you just get out the f..king van?" Sarge bellows again.

"Hey, you know me…anything to make *your* life a misery." I reply ruefully.

"Kent, help me up" I continue

I can see the perp is pinned down between 2 cars about 40 yards up. Bullets are still whizzing past and I can hear sirens round the corner. More and more lights are coming on as people in their homes are looking out their windows. Some of the residents of the street are even yelling out their windows to us…

"Hey you cops, get that guy, he's messing up our kids, selling drugs outside the school gates." They yell.

"Yeah burn his ass."

Seems like this perp is not wanted in this neighborhood.

I try to move toward the perp but Sarge grabs my arm.

"Where the heck do you think you're going? The EMS has just pulled up, you need that head wound cleaned up"

The ambulance crew gets hold of me and pulls me over to the med bus. I hear them confirm that it is just a flesh wound but it will need at least 8-10 stitches.

"You're very lucky; the bullet has left a 2 inch furrow on the top of your head. But your scalp is fine, just a lot of bleeding." One of them tells me.

"But you will have to go to the hospital, no more action for you tonight."

"Get her out of here real quick guys, that perp is still not out. It's too dangerous, don't want anyone else hurt." Sarge booms out to the crew.

Just before we leave I hear someone shout out that the gunman is down. One of the residents had shot him from a downstairs apartment.

As the ambulance pulls off from the scene, with lights flashing and sirens blasting and me in the back, I remember Lincoln.

Lincoln is the only man I've really loved; our relationship had been perfect for me…except he didn't like my being a cop. No way am I going to resign from the only job I've ever wanted to do. Still… Lincoln is the only man I ever loved. The pain killers and injections the EMS crew had given me are having an effect. I begin to drift off…

CHAPTER 3
LINCOLN CALDWELL

Wednesday April 11th
Atlanta, GA

Life has a way of always bringing you back full circle to the very place you began. Here I am, back at my Alma Mater, Morehouse College, standing in the hallway of one of the dorms and I couldn't believe it had all gone by so quickly. The memories rushed by me like the wind in a tunnel. There is no escape and I love it. I realize then that I haven't taken the time to bask in those memories of youth and irresponsibility mixed with nurturing professors and beautiful future hopefuls. The president of the current Student Government Association, Charles Berry, had invited me here because two creative writing professors at the school were using one of the books I have written, 'Capture Your Creativity'. I accepted his invitation with no qualms. After all who would have thought that I would end up as a professor of art and creative writing at Fordham University? Or that my art would be held in such high esteem throughout the New York area. Regrettably, it has been almost sixteen years since I've been back to Morehouse. I did give back monthly through the Alumni newsletter and I tell Fordham students great stories about Morehouse.

As I stroll along the hallways of Sale Hale on my way up to King Chapel, I reminisce on the days when I ran up and down these same halls. I had only just arrived in America from England a year before with my parents and little sister Lynn. I'd done my 12th grade at a High School in Roswell, Georgia and been lucky enough to get accepted into MoreHouse for my Bachelor degree program. A warm feeling of comfort and ease flows through me like a cool drink in the summer. Suddenly, I was jolted out of my surreal world by a thump on the back.

"Yo, my bad son, you alright?"

A young man had rushed out of his room and almost knocked me over.

"Yeah, I'm fine" I say as I smile at his accent and his energy.

"You lost or something?" asks the young man as he heads down the stairs.

"No, I'm going up to King Chapel."

"Oh yeah, there's supposed to be a tight speaker from Fordham in about 20 minutes, I'll be back to check that out. We get credit for that type of stuff and I need it!" remarks the young man as he smiles.

I'm almost envious of his energy and friendly demeanor. I remember that I used to be like that once. Being an artist has always been my solace. Through art I am able to find laughter and optimism. Throughout college and art school, I was always the 'cheerer-upper' of our crew. I genuinely felt as though the world was at my command and *that* energy shone through to most of the people around me. Nowadays it's as if that energy was slipping through my fingertips like sand and there is nothing I can do to stop it. Despite my continuous success in the NY art scene and the fulfillment I find in being a college professor, something is missing. I put on monthly art shows throughout the state of New York and the income is more than sufficient. All the things I set out to accomplish have materialized over the past sixteen years. Yet there is an unidentifiable emptiness that plagues me in a very painful way. I remind myself that today I am here for the students of Morehouse College and not to wallow in my own sorrows. I climb the last flight of stairs and open the door to King Chapel.

Charles Berry greets me enthusiastically along with two other SGA officers.

"Thank you so much for coming out man, traffic wasn't too bad was it?" asks Charles.

"Nah, it was cool. I'd gotten used to NY traffic 'till I went out and got a motorbike and I brought it with me."

"Aaw yeah?" says Charles with a sly grin on his round chubby face.

"That's one of the first things I'm doing when I get a real job man, I'm buying a bike!" "I'm getting a Honda 800FI VFR Interceptor."

"You got it down to a T huh, I feel you man, there's nothing like cruising the stretch on my bike! You feel a sense of serenity that's unparalleled."

We all laughed and continued our conversation on bikes as we headed toward the front of the chapel. I was handed a bottle of water and a few paper towels as I sat down and waited to be introduced. Are these butterflies I feel in my stomach? Hell no, they couldn't be! I've been speaking at public venues regularly for about twelve years now, not to mention the classes I teach. Confusion and anxiety combine and wrap themselves into a tight ball at the top of my throat. I then realize that Charles has already begun to introduce me. I smile half-heartedly as the curiosity filled faces look up at me.

"Yes brothers and sisters, none other than the Morehouse Alumnus himself, Professor Lincoln 'Linc' Caldwell!"

I stand up and walk over to the podium as I take a gulp of water.

"Thank you Charles, that intro was so good. How could you have had someone else in the program ahead of me?"

Phew! My icebreaker has worked, the crowd is chuckling and I feel more relaxed. I had anticipated a bit of a nonchalant attitude from students who were just attending this session for a class. Again a negative outlook on my part so very unlike my usual self. As I finish my speech and descend from the stage a young lady approaches me and identifies herself as Trisha, a student at the neighboring Clark University.

"Mr. Caldwell, do you have a few moments?" she asks in a shy low tone.

"Yes, certainly, what can I do for you?"

She opens her book-bag and takes out an 8 by 10 of one of my paintings.

"I'll really appreciate it if you'll sign this for me. It's a gift for my older brother, we both love your work," she says in a now more energetic voice.

I sign the back of my painting and we engage in light conversation. It turns out that Trisha is an artist majoring in English, and writing is her second love. She has followed my career since her freshman year and she is currently a junior who makes a name for herself by doing murals around the city for non-profit organizations. I give Trisha my card and tell her that she can call or e-mail me anytime. It feels wonderful to be an inspiration to someone, especially when it is as genuine as it seems to be with Trisha. My conversation with her reminds me how much I long for that type of relationship, one of a nurturing older brother, or better still, one of a father.

I take a long deep breath and suddenly I realize that I'm starving. I haven't eaten all day except for a candy bar sometime this morning. I have always been grateful for my particularly efficient metabolism, I can eat what I want, when I want and in any proportions without worrying about calories and fat intake. At 6ft 2ins, and 215lbs I have no weight gain concerns, especially since I have been this weight since I was eighteen years old.

I'd finally been able to escape from Morehouse about 2 hours ago.

"I need to chill out" I thought.

"What do I feel like eating?" I muse.

"Ah hah, Japanese food!"

I had initially developed a liking for Japanese food 6 years ago when I first started dating Ryoko. Ryoko, now that was a tumultuous relationship. Albeit caring, loving and always highly charged, it had still been a rocky road at times. I had really loved Ryoko and we still care for one another even now, 2 years after breaking up. We have remained good and close friends over the past couple of years and she has immersed herself as always, in her police duties. She's a veteran New York police officer. A member of the SWAT team, a tough cop through and through. Surprisingly we haven't spoken to each other over the past 2 days since I'd arrived in Atlanta. I wonder whether she is on some assignment. Well, enough reminiscing over Ryoko, it's time to eat. I head over to Buckhead, Peachtree Street in the heart of the city to be exact. If memory serves me well, there is a very good Japanese restaurant in the area. Several actually but I have my mind set on one in particular. I should probably run back to the hotel first, to check any messages I may have received during the course of the day. Huh, who am I kidding, do I really want to check messages in general? Or am I hoping that Ryoko might have called me. Why have I thought of her all of a sudden? After all, we're just good friends now. Aren't we? Anyway I'm here on Peachtree Street now; traffic is beginning to build up. Lot's of people milling about, some in a hurry, probably trying to catch the train at the nearby MARTA train station. I've always liked Atlanta for its Buckhead/downtown hustle and bustle. There are many sights to see, music in the air and the smell of good food. Thinking of food, shouldn't I have reached that Japanese restaurant by now or am I going in the wrong direction? Ah here I am, almost walked right passed it.

*Thursday April 12*th

Atlanta, GA

Hartsfield-Jackson International Airport always seems more like a busy little town than an airport to me. It has got to be the largest and one of the busiest Airport's in the United States. The check-in attendant said it is two miles between the north/ south terminals and the international departure lounge. I have been to JFK, La Guardia and Chicago's O'Hare, and they do not compare. Even architecturally Hartsfield is more appealing to the eye and of course I love the artwork and murals scattered around the various terminals. I hope I can settle in for a quiet snooze during this flight back to New York's JFK. Although I got a good night's sleep at my hotel in the Vinings area, I still felt a little lethargic. I suppose that could be as a result of my not working out over the past three days. I hadn't eaten dinner after my excellent meal at Bennihana yesterday evening and as far as I'm concerned it's still too early for breakfast. Never really a breakfast person, I feel human beings shouldn't start shoving food into their stomachs as early as 7 a.m.

"Would you like some orange juice or cranberry juice? The airline's flight attendant asks, bringing me out of my reverie.

"No thank you" I reply, "maybe a little later."

I settle back into my comfortable seat and close my eyes. It's great to fly business class. Images of yesterday's Japanese chef, flinging Ginsu knives up into the air and catching them on the way down with perfect precision flooded my mind. I felt almost certain that one of his fingers or a thumb would end up in the salad bowl or in the grill pan where the shrimp and calamari were sizzling! There had been loud applause coupled with an audible sigh of relief when he concluded his aerial display of razor sharp Ginsu steel without mishap. I had thoroughly enjoyed my meal and my rice wine and had returned to my hotel room. As there had been no messages from anyone, except a brief thank you from Charles Berry, I had read a little of my latest John Grisham novel and gone to bed. I wake up from my slumber just as the captain announces our descent into JFK. We'll be landing in a few minutes and I am anxious to get home.

I stroll out of the terminal and meet with the New York morning chill. I hail a yellow cab and head for East 14th Street in Manhattan, where I live. As I ride the elevator up to the 3rd floor of my building I ponder on what the rest of the week holds for me.
"I've got to call the rest of the gang to let them know I'm back in town." I say out loud.
We'll probably meet up later this evening at a jazz or comedy club. I *really* could do with some light entertainment and *just* a couple of long island teas.

CHAPTER 4
SYDNEY COLLINS

Tuesday April 17th
Manhattan, NY

Everything seems to have moved in a blur over a period of 6 days. I hadn't realized that Dad had wanted things to start taking shape this soon. Here I am in New York City, hail and hearty but mentally consumed with the almost overwhelming responsibility on my young shoulders. Dad must feel I'm emotionally stronger than I'm actually feeling right at this moment! I've been out all morning and afternoon today. Cruising in cabs and walking along 6th avenue, also known as 'the avenue of the Americas'. I have also spent the past two days researching the downtown area in Hudson Street and Silicon alley, looking for an office location for CSD. Ever since Mama had surprisingly given her blessing for me to come to New York, things had progressed at breakneck speed. I had caught Mama as she was about to leave for the airport. I had jumped into the car with her and launched into my discussion.

"Jordan just filled me in on your conversation" Mama said.

"I assume you fully understand what you are getting yourself into. It'll be a lot of hard work and determination but I agree with your father that you've got a steady head on your shoulders." She'd added.

To say I'd been a little surprised at Mama's reaction would be an understatement! Mama had never wanted me more that half an hour away from home if she could help it! Her agreeing to my going off to New York by myself, for an unspecified period of time really took my breath away.

"Thanks Mama, for your vote of confidence, I know you realize I'm quite surprised at your reaction." I'd finally responded.

"Well you really shouldn't be, after all you do know that your father and I have great confidence in your abilities."

Now here I am in The Big Apple, taking in all the sights while doing as much work as possible. I had noticed a quaint little art studio in China Town yesterday and I want to go back there; so I flag down a cab and head to Artist's Haven. It took the driver only 20 minutes to get there and I paid off the cabbie in an excited and expectant mood.

"I haven't written a poem in almost a month." I tell myself.

Of course I had been very busy with course deadlines. I'd been determined to graduate at the top and my thesis on Bio-molecular structure in plastic alloys hadn't been easy. Never-the-less I can recall occasions where I have written poems during examination periods as a means to relieve stress and relax. As I step past the shop attendant in the rear of the studio, I notice a magnificent painting on the far wall. The painting immediately draws me to it but before I can reach it, an elegantly dressed woman takes it off the wall and admires it.

"Beautiful isn't it?" I remark as I reach her side.

"I certainly agree. It is one of the most intriguing pieces I've seen in a while and it's by a local artist too." She replies.

We both admire the painting in total silence for a few moments.

"I'm definitely buying this, two thousand dollars? Hmm, not excessively priced either." She murmurs under her breath.

I immediately scan the studio for a similar painting but there isn't one. There are other works by the same artist but none that quite calls to me like this one does.

"I'll buy it off you for an additional $100!" I blurt out.

She turns around and looks at me as though I'm crazy.

"Get away from me please! This is not a flea market honey; it's a gallery. Maybe you should shop at places that are a little more up your alley!" she grinned; obviously trying to rub it in a little bit more.

People are now looking at us and I feel myself starting to get irritated.

"You don't need to get an attitude lady; I simply want the painting as much as you do. All you had to say was no thank you."

"Besides your attitude can't match mine, *if* I bring it out!" I retorted.

My loud response was very unbecoming and tacky to say the least.

"Maybe the flea market *is* more your style than you care to admit?" continues the woman.

I hear chuckles coming from various parts of the room.

"You're obviously not from around here or you'd be more careful who you mouth off to little girl!"

I looked around to see if someone else had become part of our encounter.

"Who you talking to?" I ask in all seriousness.

"Ma'am, it really isn't this serious. You are obviously attached to the painting, so by all means take it. I won't get into a fight with an old woman over a piece of canvas!" I snapped.

The woman shoots me a fierce glance, walks hurriedly over to the counter, pays for the painting and whisks herself out of the studio. Just as I'm about to leave, a man from behind the sales counter stops me.

"Young lady I apologize for your dilemma. Maybe I can be of some assistance." He says.

He introduces himself as Mack, the manager of the gallery and tells me that these "mishaps" aren't uncommon in his store. He tries to lighten the mood but it's not working. I couldn't believe the woman went off like that. However, my frustration is appeased a bit when the manager gives me the business card of the artist who had done the painting. He also scribbles the name of the painting on the back of the card and tells me that the artist probably has a copy of the exact piece. I thank the manager for his assistance and walk out of the studio. I half-expect the woman to be standing outside waiting for me.

As I open the door to my Manhattan loft, I marvel at the fact that it is actually mine. Of course I know I wasn't going to live at home forever, but this is Sydney, in New York, on her own! It was great. I really begin to feel more comfortable in the decision I have made to take on these responsibilities. I had stopped at a food store on the way home, as well as a shoe store and a few other art galleries; I was beat. I put my groceries on the counter and slumped down lazily on my couch. I lie down and realize that if I stay in this position, I will be asleep in no time. I reluctantly get up and start to unpack my groceries. I start to do my usual 'plan out the next day' routine. While doing my grocery shopping I have somewhat repented over my angry outburst at the woman in the art studio. I begin to schedule out tomorrow's activities when the phone rings, interrupting my thoughts. I don't even remember where I've put the cordless phone and I scamper around trying to find it.

"Probably Dad again," I mumble out loud as I search.

"Hello?" I pant.

"Hey Syd, how's New York babe?"

"Omar? Is that you? Dad gave you my number huh?"

My dad has always liked Omar. They even play racquet ball together from time to time.

"Yep, didn't you say you were going to call me and let me know how things are going?"

"Oh yeah, I got caught up with stuff. I was still going to call."

"Yeah sure, anyway, how goes the New York scene?"

"So far, I got lost twice, I broke a shoe heel while running for a cab, and I got into it with some woman over a painting."

"Don't have too much fun Sydney, you'll make me jealous." He says in his usual sarcastic tone.

"I know." I giggle.

"The woman said something about me being from out of town because I didn't know who I was messing with. Like she was some bigwig that everybody knows."

"Hmmm." mutters Omar.

There is a brief silence.

"You better be careful, she might've been a god-father's wife or somebody dangerous."

I laugh hysterically at Omar's comment.

"Shut up Omar, you are so ignorant!"

Omar always knows how to cheer me up. That is one of the reasons we remain friends. He has a whimsical sense of humor that is totally contagious, even when you try to fight it. We chat some more about the turns both our lives have taken. Omar will be leaving for L.A. in three days. IBM had already flown him there twice and he knows he'll love California.

"More than anything else, there are two things I'm going to miss most." remarks Omar.

"What? Home cooking and no rent?" I ask sarcastically.

"No. winter in Boston and you in shorts." he remarks in a tone that was a bit too serious for me.

"O.K Casanova you almost broke your own record. It's about to be almost three minutes since you flirted! But you just can't resist can you?"

"Nope," Omar says.

"I really will miss you Syd. You better keep in touch too. Or I'll send Mrs. Soprano from the art gallery a nasty message from you."

"I will keep in touch Omar, I mean it. Thanks for calling too. Anyway, I'm about to grab a shower and try to sort things out for tomorrow."

"Who's flirting now? You didn't have to tell me that. You trying to torture a brother or what?"

"Goodbye Omar," I smile at his relentless wit.

"Call me when you get to L.A. and give me your address and number O.K?"

"Alright Syd, later."

CHAPTER 5
SYDNEY COLLINS/LINCOLN CALDWELL

Wednesday April 18th
Manhattan, NY

It's almost seven o' clock in the evening and I am just getting home. Today at the office was hectic! Dad had flown in Mr. Whittaker from the Florida office and he has been a great help. However, he also showed me just how much work I have cut out for me. There are detailed daily reports that need to be sent to all our regional offices. There are people to hire, all of whom Mr. Whittaker and I need to interview within the next three weeks. There are employee benefits packages to be carried over, networks that need to be set up by the end of the week, and I still haven't finished decorating the office! Speaking of which, I need to call that artist about the painting I want for the office. The colors fit the décor perfectly. I sorted through my business card holder and found the card. 'Life Through Lincoln's Eyes.' Even though I stopped off at a couple of other art studios yesterday, I hadn't seen anything that I wanted for the office. Maybe this artist 'Lincoln' would have a number of other works that I'll like for the office. What is the name of his piece I had seen yesterday? the one that had caused the altercation with that woman? I looked at the back of the card again 'Serenity in Repose' hmm quite poetic, I thought. I pick up the phone and dial his number.

LINCOLN CALDWELL

My little band of close friends consists of two other guys and two women. There is Woodrow Parker (Woody as we all call him). Woody has been married to Lola for five years; they don't have any children yet but are working on it. He's an Economics lecturer at Fordham and as such is a work colleague too. Then there is Ricky

Abel, another bachelor like me. Ricky is a 35-year-old paramedic working out of the Queens area of New York. Carla Watts is a professional comedian. An interesting lady with a heart of gold almost as large as she is, she can't be more than 5ft tall but must weigh over 170 pounds. She is probably the funniest person I have ever met and is also the nicest. And of course there is Ryoko. Since I had returned from Atlanta six days ago we had all met up a couple of times. By late afternoon of the day I arrived from Atlanta, I had been able to get hold of everyone except Woody. Ricky had said he would probably be able to get hold of him a couple of hours later and had been able to do so. We had all met up for a quick meal and gone on to watch Carla perform at her usual spot. As usual with Carla we had all fallen out of our seats laughing at her hilarious performance. Even though we have heard some of the jokes before, she has a way of delivering that is so refreshing. Carla isn't one of the usual run of the mill comedians who pick out a member of the audience and tear them to pieces. So she always works extra hard with her material so not to entertain at the expense of someone else's feelings.

It's been a particularly long day today and I just feel like kicking off my shoes and settling down in front of the television. I flicked through the channels, it's 7 o'clock what can I watch? The sudden ring of the telephone startles me. Could this be one of the gang calling? I refuse to be cajoled into going out today. I'm way too tired.
"Hello, Linc speaking."
"Hi my name is Sydney I got your card from the manager over at Artists Haven in China town." the young lady on the telephone replied.
"I love one of your paintings that was there but unfortunately someone else beat me to it. Would you happen to have a copy of 'Serenity in Repose' at another studio?" Sydney continued.
This is a pleasant surprise I think to myself before responding. I also quickly try to remember if I have another copy at any studio. This particular piece has proven to be quite popular and I may have sold out all 10 copies I had made, but in any case I did have the original canvas at home.
"Hello are you still there?" She asks.

"I'm sorry, I was trying to remember if I had Serenity in repose anywhere other than the original canvas I have here at my home. I actually think the original *is* the only one I have left. I'll be glad to make a copy for you; it might just take a few days because of my schedule." I reply,

"I've just arrived in New York a few days ago and I'm decorating both my apartment and my office. I have visited a number of Art galleries and I'm particularly impressed with your work. Would you happen to have a home gallery with pieces that are not yet out on the market, which I can see? I would really love to have some original works and I don't mind paying a little extra for the privilege of having the only copies." She concludes.

"It will certainly cost more than just a little bit extra to have originals that are not to be copied. I hope you realize just how much more expensive each piece will then become. But to answer your question, yes I do have a home gallery and I will be glad to give you a guided tour. When would be a convenient day for you? Most evenings or all day Sunday would be fine by me." I respond.

"Sunday sounds good for me too, how about 1p.m? I'll be back from church by then. Should we meet somewhere or are you just going to give me your address. I live in Manhattan, are you close-by? If you are, how about if we meet at the 'Artists Haven' at 1 o'clock on Sunday, that way I will just follow you home. I'll also be able to get confirmation that you are who you say you are, from the manager of the studio. This is NY; I have to be careful you know." She says with a laugh.

I laughed too and add

"Smart lady, sounds like a good idea. That will be perfect for me too. I can't be too careful either, strange women have been known to relocate to NY too you know. So I'll see you at 1 o'clock on Sunday at the studio, I'll be at the service desk, talking to the manager."

"Okay, look forward to seeing you, bye for now." and she hangs up.

CHAPTER 6
LINCOLN CALDWELL/SYDNEY COLLINS

Sunday April 22nd
Manhattan, NY

It's 10a.m and I've just got out of bed. It looks like a beautiful morning outside, I feel like going for a ride up to Jersey or somewhere. Anywhere I can get a couple of hours of cool breeze on my motorbike. I usually take these rides by myself but on occasion in the past I have gone with Ryoko. But that was when we were still dating. I have also ridden for hours at a time with Ricky who has his own bike too. I have a Honda 800FI VFR Interceptor just like the one Charles Berry down in Atlanta wants to get and Ricky has a Kawasaki ZX-9R Ninja. Both Ricky and I thoroughly enjoy our rides into the countryside. Now that I think about it I'll give him a call to see if he feels like getting the wind in his face this morning.

"Hello, Ricky here."

"Hey Ricky my man, it's Linc, how about a Sunday morning rush on a ride? Are you up for it?"

"Sure man, as long as you don't plead for me to slow down like you did the last time." He replies.

"Ha Hah, tell you what, as long as you don't drive like a maniac I won't need to caution you and I won't need to keep an eye out for the cops either!" I countered.

"Okay Linc I'll be at your pad in 45minutes. I'll rev up my big boy's bike when I get outside, you'll hear me of course, then you can bring out your toy bike, right?"

I chuckle loudly and say

"Ricky! If I didn't have an important meeting in a couple of hours time I'd consider that a challenge 'cos that sounded like you threw down the gauntlet. See ya in 30 minutes not 45 okay?"

"Sure thing buddy I'll be there." Ricky rejoins.

Most Sunday mornings I go to church but today I feel like some other form of spiritual resonance. I love praise and worship during service but today though, I just want to hear the wind and the birds and watch the flow of the river as we ride by.

Ricky has shown up right on time, I can hear him revving his bike downstairs. I have decided that since it's such a nice day I'll ride the bike to the studio where I'm meeting Ms. Sydney. I grab both helmets and my keys and head for the elevator. I ride out from the underground parking bays and meet up with Ricky at the front of the building.

"Man, your bike is still this ugly green and white." I exclaim.

"For a professor and an artist you really are ignorant. I've told you these are the official Kawasaki racing colors." He retorts.

"Anyway whether green, red, pink, purple, or silver my 900cc engine blows away your 800cc fuel injected one." Ricky explains.

"Enough talk, let's ride."

With tires screeching we shoot off down the street heading for the Jersey turnpike.

We've been riding for over an hour and it's now past noon. I signal to Ricky to pull over.

"Let's head back; I've got to be at China Town at 1p.m remember?"

"Ok Linc, I'll just run into this gas station to get a drink, want anything?"

"Thanks Ricky, I'll have a Lucozade, any flavor will do."

"What? How long have you been in the U.S Linc? Twenty-five or twenty-six years? You know we can't get your precious British drinks just anywhere…you're gonna have to make do with a Gatorade buddy."

Five minutes later we are heading back to New York.

I pull up in front of Artist's Haven a couple of minutes before one o'clock and stride in. I can see the manager across the studio.

"Hi Mack, how are you?"

Mack had once owned Artist's Haven but had run into financial hardship and had been forced to sell. The current owner recognizes Mack's vast knowledge of art history and had asked if he would manage the studio. Mack had jumped at the opportunity. He didn't make the highest income in the city but managing the studio kept him close to his beloved art.

"Hey Linc, I'm great, I didn't expect to see you today."

"I know Mack; I'm meeting a young lady who is interested in a copy of, or the original 'Serenity in Repose'. In fact she said she got my card from you."

"Oh yeah I remember her, she was in the store a few days ago and had really liked that particular piece. She'd actually had an argument with Mrs. Van-Morrison, the Senator's wife. Remember her? She's the woman who is in here practically every other day and has probably purchased all of your works."

Just as I am about to reply I notice a beautiful young lady walk into the studio. She can't be more than twenty two-twenty three years old; around five foot ten inches tall, beautiful big eyes and a figure to die for. She starts to approach us and breaks out into a stunning smile. She can't be smiling at me I'm thinking b'cos I sure ain't never seen this beauty before!

"Hi, thank you so much for the other day." She says, looking directly at Mack.

I knew that voice immediately, this must be Sydney.

"Hey, hello to you too Miss. I'm glad I could help. Were you able to get hold of Mr. Caldwell?" Mack asks.

"Oh yeah, I certainly did. In fact he was quite nice on the phone."

"That's good because you know how these artist types can be, a little uptight or unpredi…"

I cut Mack off before he can finish, while he's still laughing.

"Excuse his bad manners." I chuckle.

"It seems *I* have to introduce myself, I'm Lincoln Caldwell and you must be Sydney!" I say, extending my hand.

She smiles and shakes my hand with a firm grip.

"Pleased to meet you Mr. Caldwell, I hope I haven't kept you waiting too long? I got here as soon as I could. I really hate to be late. Luckily it only took me fifteen minutes to get here by train."

At this point Mack decides to jump in again.

"He's only just arrived a couple of minutes ago himself. He's alright." He exclaims.

"Mack, I think there is a customer over there that needs your attention. I'll take over from here. Thank you anyway." I retort grinning.

I ask Sydney if she would like to look around the studio for a while or whether she is ready to leave. She says she is anxious to see my gallery and is ready to leave. She smiles and waves to Mack as we walk towards the exit. We step out onto the pavement and I say,

"Would you like to ride with me on my motorbike or would you like to take the train?"

I can see her hesitation before she responds.

"You're joking right?" she says smiling. Then adds,

"I've never ridden on a motorbike before and I'm not quite sure if the first time should be with a stranger!"

"I'm not a stranger any longer Sydney. We've met formally now and you *are* about to come to my apartment. Come on it'll be fun."

"Well how far are we going?"

"We are on Lafayette Street and I live on 14th street, so it's only about a fifteen minute ride. Ready?"

"Yep, what the hell let's do it, you're lucky I'm wearing jeans today. Otherwise wild horses couldn't have dragged me onto this bike." She says laughing.

We get on the bike and I make sure she has settled comfortably before we get underway. I feel a little excited and I can't understand why. One thing is for sure though, I certainly feel good with Sydney's arms wrapped tightly around me as we ride through the crowded streets of China Town.

SYDNEY COLLINS

I'm actually enjoying this motorbike ride! At first I had been a little scared especially whenever we corner. How the bike doesn't just flip us on our sides is obviously a matter of physics, probably thrust, velocity and momentum or something. Anyway this Lincoln guy seems pretty cool. I wonder what his place will look like. I'll find out in a few minutes and it'll most likely be upside down like most single men's apartments! Single man! What on earth has given me the impression that *he* is single? I don't know anything about the man and here I am contemplating his marital status! Oh boy! What's going on here? So far today I've had an enjoyable time. I had woken up at 8.30am and called to speak with Mama but Dad had said she's still not back from Haiti.

"When *is* she coming home?" I had asked.

"She'll be home next Tuesday sweetheart." Dad replied.

I had then spent the next 45minutes gisting with Dad about how the office is turning out, feedback regarding Adam Whittaker and how I'm enjoying New York.

"Dad I do not recall giving you permission to give Omar my number" I remember saying.

"Omar, who's Omar?"

"Quit it Dad, you know exactly who Omar is. That same guy that you've been trying to marry me off to? The one you play racquet ball with?"

"Oh, that Omar! Well you know how he hangs around the house like your little puppy. I took pity on the man, he was missing you. Besides I was sure you wouldn't mind."

I'm a little upset with Dad because he knows that Omar wants a relationship and that I not having it. I suppose I can't blame him entirely though, he's heard me say over and over again how much I miss Omar at times. All the same I wish Dad did not assume it is okay for Omar to know my every move. After all, our relationship has really only been a very strong friendship. Omar is just a bit too much hassle for my liking.

I'm brought back to the present as we pull to a stop in front of a brownstone building.

"Well here we are Sydney." Linc says.

I get off the bike and take in my surroundings.

"Come on Sydney; follow me we're getting on the elevator up to the 3rd floor"

"3rd floor? We don't need to get on the elevator just to go to the 3rd floor do we?" I ask.

"Nope but the stairs are pretty rickety and are being renovated. This is actually a good thing because my elderly neighbor Mrs. Grant has been campaigning for an elevator to be installed for the past 2 years!"

"It has certainly taken the owner of the building long enough then hasn't it?" I reply.

We ride up to the 3rd floor and I look around me as Linc opens his front door. He steps through the doorway and motions me in.

"You don't have to be nervous Sydney; I can assure you that I'm not an axe murderer."

"Sorry Lincoln, can I have a drink? A glass of water maybe? It'll help me relax a little."

"Sure, I'll be right back and by the way call me Linc. All my friends do" He says as he walks out of the living room.

I notice that the apartment is sparsely furnished but is quite tasteful. There is a nicely patterned 4seater couch against one wall, a couple of standing lamps, a small breakfast table with 4 chairs and two large potted plants. There's also a 6ft by 8ft Persian rug and another smaller rug, Persian also, under the breakfast table and of course the plush single chair I am sitting on. All in all it is a very nice pad and *there are no signs* of a woman living here. Surprisingly there are also none of Linc's paintings on any of the walls.

"Here you are Sydney, I didn't put any ice in it but here's some ice in a bowl if you need it."

"Thanks, I probably won't use the ice. You know Linc I've noticed that you haven't got any of your paintings on the walls, is there a particular reason for this?"

"Yes there is actually." Linc responds, as he walks over to a corner of the room.

He reaches up and pulls on a cord hanging from the ceiling (which I had not noticed earlier). Lo and behold he was pulling down a flight of steps!

"Now what have you got up there, your gallery?" I inquire.

"Yep, welcome to my humble home gallery. I have all my originals and some copies up there."

He walks back over to where I am sitting and extends his hand to pull me up.

"Thank you kind sir," I say, taking his hand.

There is a warm feeling and a tingling as I put my hand in his. Why? I can honestly tell myself that these feelings are not exactly sensual but they are definitely there! We walk up the steps. Wow! I am utterly amazed at what confronts me at the top. The attic we have reached must span the entire length and breadth of the apartment downstairs! There are paintings everywhere, 3 or 4 easels, paintbrushes and paints of every imaginable color, a computer on an antique office desk, wooden frames, rolled canvases and an extensive library. Tucked away in one corner is a lovely futon and a 42inch flat screen HDTV with both VCR and DVD players attached. There is even a small refrigerator! I walk over to look at some of the paintings and immediately see no less than seven that I want.

"These are absolutely beautiful" I exclaim.

"My pleasure" Linc responds with a great big smile on his face.

"I'm glad you like it. I spend most of my time up here reading, painting, grading my students' papers and also relaxing."

I continue walking around looking at more of his work and telling myself how talented this man really is.

"I'll take everything you've ever done," I blurt out.

Linc burst out laughing.

"You've gotta be kidding young lady! Don't get me wrong, I'm very flattered but what you just requested will cost you in the region of a few hundred thousand dollars, possibly up to a million!"

"No-one other than Mrs. Van-Morrison has ever made such a request."

"Who is she?" I ask.

He then proceeds to tell me about her and how she has purchased approximately 60% of his paintings. He then tells me he had heard from Mack that I'd met her at Artist's Haven.

"That witch is Mrs. Van-Morrison? You're right I have met her. I found her to be rude and obnoxious. She's certainly not the most pleasant person I've ever met."

Linc starts grinning again.

"What's so funny now?" I ask

"It just struck me all of a sudden, that you ladies have something in common, your taste in art!"

"Be that as it may but she's certainly an aggravating woman."

"Relax Sydney, you will probably never run into her again. Besides, Mrs. Van-Morrison can be quite amiable." Linc responds

"A rose by any other name is still a rose isn't it?" I retort.

Linc picks up a remote control and switches on the TV.

"Would you like to listen to some music?" he asks.

"No!"

I'm a little irritated at Linc's casual remarks and he seems to be standing up for that woman. Most likely he's not as concerned with her character as he is with her money. As long as she's buying his paintings why the hell should he care?

"By the way Mr. Caldwell don't call me young lady, I feel that the term is belittling, okay?"

"Yes ma'am anything you say."

That response of course only served to irritate me even more.

"You have not actually said whether or not I can buy your originals Mr. Caldwell, money is not the issue at all."

"Sorry Sydney I make it a rule not to let go of any original. I intend to keep them all for posterity. In addition, money is not my motivating factor sometimes I even give copies away for free."

By this time I am ready to leave. I am thoroughly angry and the afternoon has suddenly turned sour. "Ok then, I think I'm ready to go home now."

Linc does not say a word as he walks me down the steps leading back into the living room. I head straight for the door and open it.

"It was nice meeting you Mr. Caldwell you have a lovely gallery and an interesting apartment. I'm taking the train home; don't wanna ride on your bike"

He takes a step closer to me looks me straight in the eye and says,

"You know Sydney, we've only just met. I'm a complete professional and I don't think I have either said nor done anything that could have made you angry, so why are you upset?"

There is no denying that I am upset but I can't tell him why either, I don't even know why myself! So I just fumble for a reason. I give a deep sigh and tell him something silly.

"If you say so Sydney, anyway I'm glad you had the chance to see my work. But you taking the train home is totally out of the question. I brought you here and I'm taking you home!"

"Also, I apologize for calling you young lady. Can you go back to calling me Linc?" he concludes with a wide grin on his face.

"I don't think so! Who do you think you are? Insisting how I go home. *You* certainly don't tell me what to do. Ok?"

As he is about to speak I hold up my hand...

"I haven't finished! Is this your modus operandi? *This* is how you impress potential customers? First being rude to them then bullying them onto your bike?"

"Well I ain't impressed, damn it!" I suddenly feel stupid because I really don't know why I'm so angry. Plus Linc is just staring at me grinning.

"Anyone ever tell you how stunning you are when you're mad?" He says, still grinning.

"Let me know when you're finished 'cos *I'm* still gonna take you home." He continues.

Damn it again. What's with this guy? Talk about super confidence.

He takes my hand firmly but gently, shuts his door and leads me toward the elevator. For half a second I feel like resisting but the feeling passes, especially as he pulls me to him.

CHAPTER 7
LINCOLN CALDWELL

Sunday April 22nd
Manhattan, NY

Sydney is certainly an interesting woman but I could detect a quick temper and signs that she may be a little spoilt. I'm sure one of the reasons she has been angry is because I have refused to sell any of my originals. As it turns out she lives on East 86th Street about 15 minutes away from me. Whether or not I'll ever hear from her again is a matter of speculation. I had dropped her off in front of her building and we had exchanged a few pleasantries and that had been it. I'd wanted to kiss her outside my front door but had decided not to. Instead I had held her close for a full minute and she hadn't struggled, more like she melted in my arms. Even though she had been mad at me she hadn't pulled away, not even slightly. With her head nestled in my chest and my chin on her forehead we had stood there enjoying the moments.

Women! There were no promises to call nor have there been any questions regarding the possibility of my changing my mind. I'll just have to wait and see.

What am I going to do this evening? I wonder. I suddenly hear the phone ringing but I didn't feel like answering it.

"Who is it?" I say out loud as I walk over to the phone.

"Hello"

"Hi Linc, it's been a few days what have you been up to?"

"Hey, Woody is that you?"

"It sure is" he replies.

"How is Lola? 'Hope you've taken her to the theatre to see 'Miss Saigon'."

"You know how it is Linc. I've been too busy, besides if I can't take her either you or Carla can. In fact Carla is coming over for dinner with us tonight, how about joining us?"

"Hmm, sounds good to me…hang on a second Woody there's someone on the other line."

I switch over to the other line.

"Hello."

"Hi Linc it's me, Ryoko"

"Hello stranger. I want to speak to you but Woody is on the other line. Should I call you back in a few?"

"Alright Linc, I'll be home for another 30 minutes, say hi to Woody for me."

As Ryoko hangs up I switch back to Woody.

"That was Ryoko, she says hi."

"Thanks. So are you coming over for dinner? Bring Ryoko too."

"I don't know what her plans are Woody but I'll probably see her this evening. How about I call you later to let you know?"

"Okay Linc that's fine by me. I'll let Lola know that you and Ryoko might be coming."

"Cool, speak to you and Lola later." I hang up and decide to go up to my gallery to relax and call Ryoko from there.

As I dial Ryoko's number I again think of Sydney. There is not much I can do where *she* is concerned anyway because I don't have a contact number.

"Hey cutie, how have you been doing? Are all the criminals in NY incarcerated yet?"

"Very funny Linc but if I had my own way that would certainly be the case. Anyway how about you, Mr. Professor/Artist?"

"I've been very busy too Ryoko but I have tried a couple of times to get hold of you. I went riding this morning with Ricky before I met up with my appointment at 'Artist's Haven'. Actually that's also one of the things I want to talk to you about."

"Why? Is there something exciting happening?"

"Possibly, how about we meet up somewhere this evening and I'll tell you all about it over dinner?"

"Fair enough where do you want to eat Linc?"

"Woody and Lola have invited the whole gang for dinner but I'd rather just you and I get together, we haven't done that for a while. I'll let Woody know that we won't be at their place tonight. How about we go to that restaurant over on Hillside Avenue down in Queen's Village?"

"That's fine by me Linc; pick me up at 7p.m okay?"

"Okay Ryoko but *please* don't wear your gun tonight, wear a dress, or something else nice and feminine."

"See you later Linc, I'll try and surprise you."

I hang up and sit back in my chair looking forward to my date with Ryoko. I'm glad we've remained good friends in spite of the fact that we are no longer lovers. Both of us genuinely care for each another and I value her opinions on various issues, including affairs of the heart, as surprising as that may sound! I stretch out on the futon and close my eyes.

I wake up and slowly drag myself off the futon. It's 5.45p.m, time to get ready and leave to pick up Ryoko. I go downstairs and make myself a cup of coffee then jump into the bath for a quick shower. As I get dressed I drink my coffee. Steaming hot drinks do not go down well with me so I always drink my coffee warm. I pull on my loafers and walk toward the door, stopping to call Woody along the way.

"Hey Woody." I say as he answers his phone.

"Sorry, Ryoko and I won't be at your place tonight we've decided to meet in Queens to catch up on a couple of things."

"That's fine Linc we'll see you guys some other time, have fun."

I put the phone down and walk out of my apartment.

It only takes a short time to get to Ryoko's place. I am actually a little early. She opens her door almost as soon as I ring the doorbell. She is dressed in an exquisitely fitting dress with just the right amount of jewelry. Ryoko is also a very beautiful woman, all 5ft 5inches of her. She has the typical long black hair that most other Japanese women have but she also carries herself with the confidence of a woman who knows she can handle any man on a mental, academic and even physical level. With two college degrees, one in criminal law the other in forensic science and a second Dan black belt in Shotokan karate, Ryoko is certainly a formidable opponent or a welcome friend and ally. All this probably explains how she has excelled brilliantly in her career in the NYPD. As I stand there in her foyer I notice her looking at me expectantly.

"Well?" she asks.

"You look stunning, even more so than usual." I say smiling.

"Thanks, for a moment there I thought you weren't going to pay me a compliment after all the trouble I've taken to look this good!"

"Come on Ryoko you're not one to fish for compliments. *You know you look good enough to eat all the time*, as far as I'm concerned."

"Uh huh." she murmurs.

We crack a few jokes and talk in general for a few more minutes before leaving.

We arrive at the restaurant and I hand the keys to the valet attendant. This particular restaurant serves very good fish and is the main reason we have chosen it. Both Ryoko and I love seafood. The restaurant is also beautifully decorated and tonight they have both pianist and singer belting out old Bobby Womack favorites. Although not fully packed, there are at least 20 other diners here tonight. In my opinion that's a good number; I don't like overly packed restaurants.

Our meal was perfect and of course we had both thoroughly enjoyed it. I had eaten Alaskan snow crab legs, grilled catfish, scallops and a variety of steamed vegetables. Ryoko had gone with 2 broiled lobsters and a ton of grilled shrimps. Dessert though was a no brainer…We both had strawberry cheesecake and coffee. As we settle into our cups of coffee I decide it's time to tell Ryoko about Sydney. I go ahead and tell her everything, from when I had received the first phone call from Sydney to when I dropped her off at home.

"Hmmm, interesting, it sounds like you're hooked Linc so when are you going to call her?"

"Can't do that, I don't have her number."

"You don't have her number? Unbelievable! You let a potential customer who can possibly spend thousands of dollars slip away? What's the matter with you Linc?"

I now feel a little flustered at Ryoko's remarks. Of course she was right though. Even for business reasons alone I should have asked for her number, funny enough it totally slipped my mind at the time. The waiter came over and I paid and left a tip as we got up to leave the restaurant.

"It slipped my mind." I said.

"Well maybe she'll call sometime soon. If she does don't let her get away incognito again, right?"

"Yeah right." I answer rather sheepishly.

Ryoko burst out laughing

"You should see the expression on your face, it reminds me of my pet poodle after I tell her off!!" she says, still laughing.

"I'm glad *someone's* getting some laughs out of this." I chuckle.

It had started to drizzle lightly outside and a full moon illuminated the street. Two street lights provide additional light and the flow of cars driving past the restaurant make it a busy night. It's only 9p.m anyway and it's NY, of course it'll be busy. Suddenly we hear a woman scream!

"Over there Linc, look! Across the road about 20 yards up."

I too could see the screaming woman. A man is dragging her back into the house with his arm around her throat and he's threatening her with a gun.

"Call for back up!" Ryoko shouts.

She immediately lifts up the hem of her dress and pulls out the gun she usually carries strapped to her thigh. I can't believe this is happening right in front of us. I also immediately felt sorry for the perpetrator because with Ryoko on the scene he's certainly in for a *baaad* day. I didn't need to call the cops. Someone from the crowd of 12 or more people already gathered, had called. A squad car with two officers came screeching to a halt right in front of the restaurant. They jump out, guns drawn and race across the road. I can hear one of the officers call Ryoko by name, so they must be from the same precinct or have worked together before. She briefs them about what she has seen and I can hear sirens from other squad cars speeding to the scene. Meanwhile the man has succeeded in dragging the woman into the house and we can all still hear her screaming. There are now additional voices yelling and screaming in the house, children's voices to be exact.

The crowd is getting larger and you can feel the tension in the air. Five other squad cars pull up and more cops spill out into the street.

Some of the officers pull out their M16 rifles from the trunk of the squad cars. The crowd is now noisy and the cops are trying to move us back into the restaurant and other open shops.

"Get back, get back inside!" They yell at us.

A few bystanders attempt to get closer to the action, me included. The cops don't take kindly to this and they push us back roughly.

"You trying to get hurt buddy?" one of them says to me as he shoves me to the side.

"Hey! Take it easy, that one is with me, back off!" yells Ryoko.

There is the sharp sound of breaking glass as the man with the gun smashes an upstairs window and suddenly there is chaos as he starts firing shots at anyone he can see outside. We all dive for cover. Ryoko is making her way back to me using the parked vehicles as shields.

"Are you okay Linc? It looks like we've got either an angry husband/boyfriend or some other type of crazy loonytoon here. What a night this is turning out to be huh!"

"Keeping your company is always exciting and dangerous isn't it cutie? At this rate we're going to be here all night! And I thought you weren't supposed to have your gun on you tonight."

"Good thing I didn't listen to you huh! If I had I'd be up the creek without a paddle" she says with a wide grin.

I have to agree with her. This woman certainly knows her job! There is another shot just as the front door swings open. The woman comes running out, straight into the arms of one of the officers.

"My kids my kids" she screams.

"You've got to get my kids out of there. He's got our six kids in there and he's threatened to kill them all and then commit suicide…"

Ryoko says her apologies to me and makes her way back across the street. There are now more than ten cop cruisers on the street, in the immediate vicinity and maybe twice as many officers. There's also an ambulance on the scene. Things are shaping up for a bad night. I call Woody and tell him what is going on.

"Man that's something. Are you and Ryoko okay?"

"We're fine Woody. You know her; she's right in her element. Listen I'll keep you posted gotta go."

The man in the house is firing more shots but the police can't fire back because of the kids. I could see Ryoko taking charge and it seems she is about to implement some strategy or something. One of the cops has handed her a bulletproof vest, which she immediately puts on. I am sure a police negotiator must be on his way by now so what is Ryoko up to? There's still a lot of commotion coming from inside the house and the kids' screams are beginning to sound more desperate.

It's now obvious! They have decided not to wait for the negotiator! With the children's lives at stake every second counts! Two of the officers are using the portable battering ram to smash the door in order to gain entry. Ryoko and three more officers are poised to rush in as soon as the door gives way. My heart is pounding faster and faster and I suddenly remember why Ryoko and I had split up. This kind of constant drama with the distinct possibility of death is a little too much for my system. I am by no means a coward but not knowing whether or not a loved one is going to come home from work…? The officers have finally smashed the lock. The signal's given and Ryoko and three other officers storm into the house. Immediately following, there is rapid gunfire; at least 16 to 20 shots are fired then sudden deathly silence! The silence lasts a good 30 seconds before the all-clear signal is given by one of the cops that had stormed the house. This whole scenario has lasted approximately 25 minutes a lot shorter than I had anticipated. I had been prepared to be on the scene for at least 3 or 4 hours! The Para-medics are running into the house. Where is she? Where is Ryoko? I can see her! She is speaking into a 2-way radio and waving away the helicopter that was hovering overhead. It takes her another 10 minutes before she can make her way across the street to where I am. She looks very depressed as she walks over.

"We were too late Linc. That sonofabitch had already taken out two of his kids before we got to him. His 6 or 7-month-old baby and the two year- old, that animal!" she swears.

The incident suddenly takes its emotionally toll on her and she breaks down in my arms and cries.

"I'm sorry cutie, it's a good thing that you were in the neighborhood things could have been a lot worse."

I comfort her. I hold her close till she calms down. She tells me she'll be making a report over at the precinct and would ride there in one of the squad cars.

"I'll come along too." I tell her. "That way I can take you home afterwards."

"Thanks Linc. It will most likely take about half an hour, are you sure you can wait?"

"Of course, just point out the squad car you'll be riding in and I'll follow."

We are finally on the way home, it's nearly 10.30p.m and the paper work at the precinct had taken an hour. Most of the cops at the precinct consider Ryoko a hero. They have worked with her over the years and respect her managerial skills as well as her police skills. I also find out though that some of the other officers think that she is sometimes a little reckless.

"Are you scheduled to work tomorrow?" I ask her.

"Yeah. I'll be working the 2nd shift so I'll be able to get a good night's sleep before I need to get to work."

"Good."

We arrive at Ryoko's place and go in.

"I'll stay for a while before I leave; I want to make sure you're completely okay"

"Linc! I'm not a rookie remember? I've been in similar situations in the past and I can handle myself, I'm fine."

"Yeh sure, then why did you break down and cry?"

"I don't know, maybe it was the babies or because it all happened so fast. I just thank God that I'd had some intuition that there wasn't enough time for a negotiator."

"You're right about that Ryoko."

We both go silent for a while. I get up and make us both a drink while she curls up on the sofa. Two minutes later I walk back in with the drinks only to find her fast asleep. I go into her bedroom and bring out a blanket, cover her up and give her a kiss on the forehead. I step out into the foyer of the apartment then pause.

"I don't think I want to leave her alone tonight" I tell myself.

I quietly go back into Ryoko's apartment jamming the door shut.

I slip my loafers off and walk over to her on the sofa. I lie down, snuggling up to her and she molds her body comfortably next to mine.

"Thanks for coming back Linc; you always know what I need." She whispers sleepily as she holds me even tighter.

CHAPTER 8
RYOKO YOKOZUNA

Sunday April 23rd
Manhattan, NY

"6 a.m. wow, I must have been really tired. I didn't even hear Linc leave. When did he leave?" I ask myself sleepily.

My mind immediately returns to last night's drama outside the restaurant. I'm always prepared for the unexpected, well almost always. I briefly dwell on a couple of life threatening incidents of the past. One being the day some bad guy had given me a small dent in my head from a gun shot. Said gun shot would definitely have killed me if it had been a millimeter lower. I was *real* lucky that day!

I slowly drag myself off my sofa and head to my kitchen. I plug in my coffee maker, open my refrigerator looking for some strawberry yoghurt and grab the closest one.

As I leave the kitchen heading for the bathroom I again remember last night.

The meal with Linc had been cozy, nice and exciting but the evening had really turned out to be exciting in a dangerous way.

I recall shouting out to the first two of my colleagues to join me at the scene.

"Hey Matt, Joe, you guys clear the street over there get those civvies back into their homes. I'll take care of this side of the street."

The guy with the strangle hold on the woman's neck has just succeeded in dragging her back into the house. We could all hear her screams mixed in with kids' screams as well.

There are too many people on the street, too many cars and way too few police back up.

I've got to get more officers here fast. I run across to Matt's parked cruiser and grab the radio mic in the car.

"Hey dispatch, this is Lieutenant Yokozuna, badge number 3339 out of the 21. We've got a hostage situation here at 1705 Landon Street, 50 yards down from the Chevron gas station. Kids are hostage too, perp is armed and dangerous. We need back up right now and send the Med bus too." I shout into the mic.

"Matt" I yell across the street.

"We've got to clear this street faster, that guy could run out the house shooting at anything that moves."

I run over to Linc at the same time as 3 other squad cars pull up with screeching tires.

"Hey Linc you've got to get back into the restaurant with the others, it's unsafe out here."

"With this many people and the bad lighting……I don't want anyone catching a stray bullet. Come on Linc get moving"

The sudden sound of breaking glass causes me to turn around and run back towards the house. I turn and yell at Linc to duck. At that moment the gunman begins firing through the window at us. A minute or so later the woman comes running out of the house screaming.

"My kids, my kids."

One of the officers grabs her and rushes her to safety behind the newly arrived ambulance. We can't return fire because we know that there are children in the house plus we don't have a clear shot of the perp anyway. I now have at least 10 cops with me, the ambulance crew and a chopper circling overhead. I can hear more squad car sirens in the distance. It is time to take decisive action; I'm not giving this perp a chance to…

"Darn it…"

A shot smashes the side mirror of the white Lexus SUV I'm crouching next to.

"Is this chump aiming at me? Hell no, that's it!" I grunt to myself.

"Hey Matt, Joe, grab the ram out your cruiser we're going in. Move it guys…we're going in right now" I tell them.

I grab hold of another uniformed cop.

"Hey what's your name…Grazonni? Ok let's go, follow me. Soon as we smash the lock we're going in. Ok?"

"Sure you wanna do that?" Grazonni asks me.

"You deaf or something buddy? That wasn't a suggestion come on damn it."

The four of us make our way cautiously toward the front door of the house. Grazonni and I take position 3-4 feet from the door, using the thick wooden frame as a shield. Matt and Joe begin using the ram to batter at the door lock. The gunman continues to fire out of the small window to our left. Judging by the size of the window it seems he's probably in the bathroom or kitchen. Moments later the lock smashes and the four of us rush in; guns drawn ready to fire.

The walls of the front room seem to be painted red. The couch and recliner are both turned over; two large Oriental standing lamps are smashed and lying on top of the green ottoman. Several wall paintings and photographs are lopsided and there seems to be red paint splattered across the 40 inch television also lying on its side. The whole room is a mess and there is broken glass all over the floor but the big shock stares us right in the middle of the room. The gunman is struggling with two youths; he has a revolver in one hand and a machete in the other. But the worst sight is the bodies of two baby girls lying along the right wall to our immediate right. There is blood all over them, soaked into their clothing and pooled around their bodies. They look obviously dead. The larger of the two bodies looks to be no more than 2 years of age but her head is nearly decapitated. The smaller child has two gunshot wounds to her chest and her left arm has been hacked. Like a bombshell I suddenly realize that what I had thought to be red paint is actually *blood* splattered all over the front room wall.

Two other kids, boys about 8 and 10 years old are huddled in the far corner of the room away from the struggling gunman and the 2 youths. The gunman looks like he's high on drugs. Close up I can now see his wild eyes, bearded unkept face and filthy shirt and jeans. He has only one shoe on and the other foot is heavily bandaged with a blood soaked hand towel.

It only takes me a second or two to take all this in.

"Drop your weapons right now." yells Joe who is slightly behind me to my left.

"Hey boys get on the floor immediately" I yell

The youths immediately drop to the floor and so do the two young boys huddled in the far corner.

A second later the gunman raises his gun and begins firing.

Simultaneously I fire off four rounds center mass, as Matt, Joe and Grazonni fire off several rounds too. I hear Joe grunt, drop his weapon and fall back against the door frame. Matt swears something unholy…as I fire off two more rounds that all slam into the perp's chest. Perp goes down in a heap after taking what must be at least 15 shots to his chest and stomach. Times like this I wish I still carried my trusted Glock 21 .45AUTO. Two rounds from me alone would have put his ass down permanently!

I look down at Joe. He's taken one round in his right shoulder just on the edge of his Kevlar vest but he'll be fine.

Matt checks the vital signs of the fallen gunman, nods his head at me to confirm he's dead. I move over to the two babies and confirm the same, both are dead. The two boys and the two youths are shaking on the floor, obviously still scared. This is an experience that they'll never repeat, I'm sure. Seems they have witnessed the murder of their two baby sisters. After checking the whole house……

"Give the all clear Matt."

"Ok, Lieutenant." He replies.

"Hey Lieutenant, you stopped one in your vest, didn't you feel the shell hit?" Grazonni asks.

I look down at my vest surprised. There *is* a round lodged in my vest. Huh, I hadn't felt it. I yank the vest off and hand it to Grazonni. It has done its job, now I need to replace it.

A whole crowd of cops and EMS guys enter the front room as I kneel next to Joe.

"Hey Joe old buddy, how are you feeling?" I ask with concern

"I'm good Ryoko, just won't be playing any tennis for a while." He grins.

"Too bad, it'll give Matt time to practice and kick your ass when you're fit again." I laugh.

"Hey you guys, someone take care of the kids and the rest of you get the hell out of my crime scene. Where's CSU?" I yell.

I stroll back out into the cool breeze and look for Linc.

I see him in the distance but first I have to hand down some instructions and assign some tasks.

Ten minutes later I make my way to rejoin Linc.

CHAPTER 9
SYDNEY COLLINS

Saturday April 28th
Manhattan, NY

How could this happen? Here I am rushing around my apartment like a headless chicken. I can't believe I overslept; it is now 7.15 am and I'm supposed to be at the airport at 7.30. I should have booked a cab last night like I had initially planned but I had been sure I would wake up on time, say around 6am. I practically run out of the apartment and down the one flight of stairs. It takes another five minutes to flag down a cab and I finally settle in the back seat.

"JFK please, as fast as you can, I'm supposed to meet my mother at the arrivals gate in six minutes."

"Can't do it in six minutes ma'am" the cabbie says, "but I can get you there in less than twenty it's Saturday morning remember?"

"Alright then, just get me there as quickly as you can and I will make it worth your while."

I relax a little and think of the conversation I'd had with Mama two days ago. She had called me at the office to tell me that she was in North Carolina. She had gotten back home to Boston on Tuesday just like Dad had said but had only stayed two days. She had gone on to Winston Salem, North Carolina to see my Grandmother. Grandma had moved back there from Georgia around the same time Mama had got married and moved to Boston. This was all when I was only three years old. At the time, Mama's older siblings, her two older brothers and two older sisters were either in drug and alcohol rehab or in jail. Actually the last I heard from Mama about any of her family except grandma, was that her two older brothers had died in a gunfight with the police during a drug raid. And one of her sisters is still in prison for the attempted murder of her own son. As to the whereabouts of her other sister, she has no idea. I have never met any of my relatives on my mama's side but one thing was certain, she has been determined to escape the circumstances of her upbringing and family and has succeeded! It's why I can forgive many things about her that I don't like. I have often voiced my desire to meet my one cousin from my mother's side but she will not even entertain the thought, let alone my trying to find him.

As I look out the cab window at the Saturday morning traffic and the clouds in the sky I reminisce over how Mama and Dad met. Apparently I was only two years old at the time. It had happened in Atlanta Georgia; Mama had been on her way to work early one morning on I285 and had been rear ended by this distinguished looking man. They had exchanged insurance details and telephone numbers and one thing had led to another. A couple of months down the line a relationship had developed. The distinguished looking man turned out to be my father. Although I have known since I was six that I am adopted, I have never referred to or seen Dad as anything other than a biological father. I love him deeply he's always been such a loving man, kind, generous and always there when you need him. He is the only father I've ever known. I have never been able to get any useful information about my biological father from either Mama or Dad. He could be dead or worse. Maybe Mama doesn't even know who he is!

"Nearly there, ma'am, I'll say less than two minutes more"
The cabbie breaks into my thoughts, one minute later we *are* here. I pay the driver and run into the terminal. The time is 7.43am I am thirteen minutes late. As I run toward the arrival gate I can see Mama and her luggage ahead of me. Many a time her attractiveness has struck me. I have been told that I am beautiful but in my opinion, Mama is a knockout. Even though I am 5ft 10in tall Mama is still taller by 2 inches. She is 6ft tall, has short hair (she always keeps her hair short) a beautiful figure and I get my eyes from her. We don't really look alike but we both have the same large eyes. I catch up to her.
"Hi Mama." I shout.
She turns around and gives me a hug

"Hello sweetheart you look well thank goodness but do you have to make a scene, shouting out loud like that?"

I give Mama a great big smile, thinking to myself only *my* mother would say that to her daughter, whom she hasn't seen for three weeks.

"I'm just pleased to see you and I don't care who else knows." I say still smiling.

We leave the airport and head for home.

"Your father has told me that things are coming along quite well at the office."

"Yes they are and Adam Whittaker has been a blessing too. There are six staff members on board now, all the computer networks have been set up and we've been in daily contact with the other offices."

"Sounds like you've really been busy Sydney. When are you coming home for the weekend?"

"I've only been here three weeks Mama and even though Adam and I have achieved a lot there's still a great deal to be done. As far as Boston is concerned I don't know when I'll go. Why don't you and Dad visit me soon?"

"Hmm, I'll speak to your father maybe we'll do just that, by the way have you found a good church yet?"

"Not yet Ma, I asked a couple of the staff but none of them go to church which is a shame really."

"Why is it a shame? Oh never mind. I don't want another lecture from you regarding me and your father giving our lives to Christ, as you term it."

"One of these days you'll understand Mama and as I've told you before, it's one of my missions to bring you to the Lord."

The cab pulls up in front of my apartment and the cabbie helps us with Mama's suitcase. Once upstairs Mama says she wants to take a nap. I take her to my bedroom and leave her to relax while I go to the living room to conclude a poem I was writing. It doesn't take me long to realize that I'm a little sleepy myself so I stretch out on the couch and take a nap too. It is my rumbling stomach and the smell of food that wakes me up. Mama is in the kitchen preparing one of my favorite meals, gumbo. The time is 11.30a.m I'd been asleep for nearly three hours. How Ma had found the necessary ingredients is a mystery.

"Ah ha sleeping beauty awakes." Mama says

I smile as she busies herself in the kitchen.

"You know that I've missed your cooking too Mama, *I think* that a once a fortnight visit from you, just so you can whip up your culinary magic would be great. What do you say?"

"There's nothing I cook that you can't cook just as well Sydney."

"Not quite Ma." I said.

A short while later we are eating and generally having a nice mother/daughter get together. After our meal Ma tells me she would like to visit the office. We decide to walk a little before getting a cab.

CSD is located on the 4th floor of the office building. As we ride the elevator Mama comments on the Manhattan skyline and compares it to downtown Boston.

"One of the things I miss about Georgia is all the greenery, the hills and mountains and the lack of excess concrete surrounding you."

I agree with her as we reach CSD's main doors. I open the doors and we walk in. Mama spends the best part of 30 minutes looking around without saying much. Finally she says

"Something is missing but I can't quite put my finger on it."

"It's probably the absence of art on the walls." I reply.

I then launch into my search for art, how I have been into a number of art galleries but have only liked the work of a Mr. Lincoln Caldwell. I go on to tell Ma about our meeting and about my altercation with Mrs. Van-Morrison.

"My, you've been busy sweetheart. Why haven't you called Mr. Caldwell?

It seems to me that you would have purchased some of his paintings by now especially since you like most of his work."

I explain that he has refused to sell me any of his originals and I have therefore decided not to buy anything at all from him.

"Sydney! Don't tell me you are cutting off your nose to spite your face. It doesn't make any sense at all." Ma exclaims.

"Give me the man's number I'd like to see his studio myself!"

In the mood Mama is in, I know there was no arguing with her so I give her Linc's card, 'Life through Lincoln's eyes'.

"What's this on the back of the card? Serenity in Repose." Mama asks.

"That is the name of the piece I like the most." I reply.

"Rather poetic I think."

"That's exactly what I thought too Mama. One of the questions I forgot to ask him is how he came about choosing that name for the painting." I tell Mama.

She immediately picks up the phone and begins dialing.

"Hello, may I speak to Mr. Caldwell?" I hear her say.

"This is Mrs. Collins, Sydney's mother………thank you. Would it be possible for me to see your gallery also? Sydney has told me she was very impressed with your work………I can? Thank you so much…5p.m this afternoon…we'll both be there. Thank you once again."

"Mr. Caldwell has agreed to show us his gallery at 5p.m today is that alright with you?"

"Yes Mama. It's really just around the corner from home, so we can leave home say around 4.30p.m"

We leave CSD and arrive back at my place 20 minutes later.

CHAPTER 10
LINCOLN CALDWELL

Saturday April 28th
Manhattan, NY

Now that's what I call a surprise call! Sydney's mother! I think about the fact that I would be seeing Sydney again in just three hours. I feel excited again just like the first time I had met her. I wonder whether I should cancel my other arrangement for this afternoon. The gang is supposed to be coming over to my place for our regular chess and home cooked dinner session. Why we still make a tournament out of the chess sessions I don't know, because Ricky always wins anyway. None of the rest of us is in his league. Ricky is actually internationally ranked as a Master; he often travels to Europe and around the US to play in tournaments that often have winner's purses up to $75,000 or more. Maybe it would be a good idea not to cancel, that way everyone will get to meet Sydney and I'll be able to get their opinion of her. I decide to leave the arrangements as they are. The gang will all be here by the time Sydney and her mother arrive.

    3.55pm. the doorbell rings, I know that one of the gang has arrived, probably Woody and Lola, they are usually the first to show up. I open my front door and just as I had suspected *it* is Woody and Lola.
    "Hi guys."
    "Hey Linc, I'm still a bit mad at you for going off with Ryoko instead of both of you coming over for dinner last week. To make matters worse you haven't even stopped by to apologize in person." Lola says glaring at me, grinning.
    I laugh out loud!
    "Stop pretending Lola, both your hubby and I know that you can never get angry at me, at least not for more than a few seconds!"

We all laugh as they come in. I apologize all the same because Lola is such a lovely person and it is the second time I have cancelled dinner at their place. All three of us start talking about the police incident I had witnessed last week. A few minutes later the doorbell rings again. This time it's Carla.

"Hey how are you Linc? Long time no see." She says.

I give her a big hug, take her hand and lead her inside. Carla asks Woody to pull down the steps for her, she wants to go straight upstairs to listen to a new jazz CD she had bought on the way over. With music playing and Lola in the kitchen cooking I feel a sense of well-being. My best friends surround me and life couldn't be much better. The only thing missing is a relationship that would possibly lead to marriage and maybe a couple of kids! I go upstairs to join Carla and thereby miss the arrival of Ryoko and Ricky. Woody, Lola, Ryoko and Ricky all came upstairs to listen to music for a while. I have to go and leave a note on my door for Sydney and her mother because there is a tendency to not hear the door-bell when I'm in the attic.

"Pawn to king four." Lola says to Carla.

"Hmm you're so predictable Lola. You've opened with white and that move every single time."

"Well we'll see whether or not you can take advantage of that knowledge. I think I've got your number Carla."

Woody of course interjects in support of his wife.

"Hey Carla will you be quiet and let the woman concentrate?"

Everybody laughs. Historically Lola beats Carla more often than not, probably with around a 7 out of 10 advantage. Chess for all of us, including Ricky, is a game we all love. It's also relaxing at least *we* all believe so.

"Linc I'll get it." Ricky says in response to the doorbell.

I have informed the gang that I am expecting additional company and I have told Ryoko in particular who it is. Ricky opens the door, says his greetings and motions for Sydney and her mother to come in. I meet them just as they step through.

"Hi Sydney, good to see you again."

I turn to her mother and introduce myself to her as Linc.

"Pleased to meet you Linc, please call me Valerie." She responds.

I introduce Sydney and Valerie to the rest of the crew. Carla offers them drinks while Lola brings them some hor'd'ourves. We all sit around getting acquainted for 15 minutes before I suggest to Valerie that she comes up to see my gallery. She says she is so we go upstairs. Sydney stays downstairs, engrossed in some lively controversial issues with Carla and Ryoko. Out of the corner of my eye I see Ryoko give me a smile and a covert thumbs up. I try not to look pleased as I catch up with Valerie. I had spent a few minutes rearranging the gallery during the week and had also finished a painting I had been working on for a while. Valerie walks around very slowly, taking her time with each painting, savoring the works like a true connoisseur.

"You've certainly got a lot of talent Linc. I can see what Sydney means when she told me she thinks you're the most talented artist in NY."

"Thanks Valerie."

"Have you ever considered taking your work international?" she asks.

"I have some friends in Boston who travel around the world and are very much into art. A couple of them are actually looking for investment opportunities in the art world."

I think for a minute before responding.

"I have to think about it some more. If truth be told I've considered it before, but I'm very busy as it is with my college responsibilities as well as my paintings. Money has never been my motivating factor, this allows me to use whatever spare time I have exactly as I please."

"You've got a point there Linc, being happy at what you do is certainly paramount. I've seen quite a few of your pieces that I would like to buy; I'll point them out to you."

By the time we conclude our business Valerie has bought $25,000 worth of paintings. She sits down on the futon and we talk for a while. Ryoko and Sydney come upstairs to look for us.

"You guys seem to be getting along real well. Did you find anything you like Valerie?" Ryoko asks.

"I certainly did and I've bought a few too."

"I'd say *more* than a few Ryoko. Valerie has bought $25,000 worth."

"I'm going to have to make two trips to deliver them." I add.

"*Great* Ma, which ones did you pick? Did you pick Serenity in Repose?"

Serenity in Repose *is* one of the paintings Valerie has chosen, which pleases Sydney somewhat. I make arrangements to deliver the paintings within the next 48hours and Valerie and Sydney prepare to leave. Valerie and I continue our conversation regarding international expansion and Ryoko and Sydney join in. In fact Woody, Lola and Ricky all get involved. By the time Sydney and Valerie reach the door everybody thinks it is a good idea. The gang says their goodbye and I walk mother and daughter to the elevator. The elevator doors open as I shake Valerie's hand.

"I hope to speak with you again sometime soon." I tell her.

"Sydney I'm glad you came along too, I was hoping that I'd hear from you but because I didn't have your number there was nothing I could do, unless you called me. I'll call you tomorrow. Is that okay?"

She glances at her mother briefly before responding.

"Sure, why not. I'll speak to you tomorrow then. Goodbye."

We shake hands and they get into the elevator as I turn and walk back to my apartment.

CHAPTER 11
SYDNEY COLLINS

Thursday May 11th
Central Park, NY

I have been so tied up with office work over the past ten days, with issues like payroll supervision, hiring of the IS manager, purchases and completion of the décor, that I've turned down Linc's two dinner invitations. But I've finally agreed to go out with him tonight. Without Adam's help I wouldn't even have been able to meet him here tonight! Adam has become a permanent feature of CSD New York. A replacement for him at the Fort Lauderdale office has been hired because I requested it. He has become invaluable to me.

    I had mentioned Linc's dinner invitations to Mama and she had voiced a few concerns about my dating him, before she went back to Boston. She had answered my phone a few times and had spoken to him. She knows I am attracted to him because I actually told her. Mama's major concern though is our age difference. She has guessed Linc to be in his mid to late 30's. Left to me his age is no problem at all! I've always been attracted to older men anyway and I had reminded Mama that I had always said *just that*! Of course, she disagrees and to further complicate matters she is in cahoots with Dad regarding Omar. Well nobody, not even Dad, is going to tell me who I go out with, especially not at my ripe old age of 22! Besides I'll be 23 in November and even *they* know that aside from my inherent level headedness, I have a high standard of accountability in every thing that I do.

    Well here I am, waiting for Linc and looking forward to a nice evening. Hopefully it'll turn out that way.
There's a tap on my shoulder and I swing round startled.
"Hello beautiful." Linc says grinning from ear to ear.

"How did you sneak up on me without me hearing you?"

"Is that the best greeting you can give me?" he says still grinning.

"For now it is sir." I reply, smiling as well.

He takes my hand and we begin to walk through the park. The evening is cool and slightly breezy.

"I can walk unaided you know, you don't have to hold my hand Linc." but I find myself moving closer to him!

"Sssh Sydney, I like holding your hand." he replies chuckling.

Well, well, well what have I found here? A sensitive take-charge guy, I like that! Now all I need to know for the moment is whether or not he's Christian.

I had found out from Linc earlier on in the week that he had been very busy too. One of his post-grad students over at Fordham University had got himself into trouble with the law. Apparently he had beaten up his girl friend that had a drug problem. She had repeatedly and systematically sold off all his belongings to finance her drug habit. The police had arrested him and he had been arraigned to appear before a judge. Linc had gone to court to vouch for him as a character witness. When I challenged him over it he had told me that the guy is an excellent student. But more importantly, his beating his girlfriend is completely out of character, so much so that two other lecturers at the university had also gone to his aid.

"Still not hungry Sydney?" Linc asks.

"Hmmm, I can do with a light dinner, maybe a salad or a small sandwich."

"There's a place across the park called Terrace on the Park. We can grab a bite to eat there."

"Okay but let's walk for a few more minutes this is my first time in Central Park."

I feel very much alive and comfortable in Linc's company. Even when we walk in silence there seems to be a mutual enjoyment; it feels as if we've known each other for years instead of just a few weeks. Our attraction to one another is obvious. Things between us are progressing very quickly but I am game. In comparison, my friendship with Omar had started off very slowly. We had been course mates throughout our sophomore and junior years. It was only during our senior year that we had become very close and even though we had gone on a couple of dates it had remained platonic. Linc and I finally decided to grab a bite to eat. I order a light salad while Linc just has a coffee.

"What did you think of my friends Sydney? You met all of them at once you know."

"I liked them, particularly Ryoko and Carla. Carla is hilarious; she also remarked that you and I kinda look alike."

"Really? That woman must need glasses or something." He laughs.

I go on to tell Linc how I'd gotten along very well with Ricky. I play chess also and of course Ricky had wanted to know how well I played. He found out quickly enough that I'm only a social player. All in all I had really liked them all.

"What was the excited discussion you had with Ryoko about?" Linc asks.

"Oh! We were discussing the virtues of being a Christian in direct relation to sexual intercourse before marriage."

"How on earth did you guys get onto such a topic so soon?"

"Easy, I bet you know as well as I do that sex, politics and religion are the most controversial and easily argued topics." I reply smiling.

"By the way Linc, what is your opinion on the issue?"

He takes his time responding and I have to nudge him sharply to let him know that I am still waiting for his reply.

"Hey girl that hurt."

"How long is it going to take you to answer my question? It's been 10 minutes." I say.

"Okay, okay, *I* think that it depends on the individual's beliefs. If a person's religion or personal ethics dictates it then so be it. Personally I feel that making love with a loved one, whether married or not, is an expression of that love also. As far as my religious beliefs are concerned, I'm not a born-again Christian but I am a regular churchgoer. I was brought up in both the Baptist and Methodist churches."

Linc's views are obviously not the same as mine. It was clear he was not a Christian in the same sense that I am. Even though I have been a Christian for only a year I've certainly grown spiritually and matured in my outlook toward many day-to-day occurrences. That's why I get so angry with myself whenever I lose my temper or act in a way that I consider immature.

I often recall the day I was invited to a church meeting. There had been a well-known Minister preaching that morning and I had thoroughly enjoyed the experience. The praise and worship songs had been spirit moving and the sermon uplifting. There had been an alter call and I had answered whole-heartedly. Since then I pray often, read my bible frequently and listen to certain types of Christian music. Compared to some of the other Christians I'd met on campus, I'm just a baby. They've told me I should attend church every Sunday and also buy more Christian literature. Of course I do not agree with everything they say but I do feel that I have not fellowshipped with other Christians for a couple of months now. I have not yet found a church here in New York and have not yet met any practicing Christians either. But hey, life goes on and I intend to enjoy it, nowhere in the bible does it say we shouldn't!

Linc has been watching me as he drinks his coffee. I tell him about my childhood, about the fact that Mr. Collins adopted me, that my name on my birth certificate is *Sydney Richmond*, that I don't know anything about my real father but that I would not exchange anyone for my adopted father. I also tell Linc about my religious experiences over the past one year and how I have come to be in New York at this time. I even tell him about Omar. What I did *not* tell Linc is that my Ma does not approve of my dating him and Omar is most definitely jealous. Omar had called from Los Angeles a few days ago. I had told him about Linc and he practically hit the roof! We had argued and had a big fight over it. I do not appreciate Omar telling me that I belong to him or that I'm just a little girl about to be swallowed up by some New York predator! Even after I had taken the time to explain who and what Linc did for a living, Omar had still been very condescending and insulting. I had eventually slammed the phone down on him after telling him to never call me again. He'll probably call and speak to my Dad but at this point I don't care. Linc clicks his fingers in my face to bring me back to the present.

"Hello."

"I'm sorry Linc, I got lost in my thoughts for a moment. I was remembering some unpleasant things that happened recently."

"Wanna talk about them?"

"No but thanks. I've told you too much about me already." I reply seriously.

"Why am I opening up to you so soon? I feel as if I have known you all my life."

He smiles at me and says,

"That's fine by me Sydney. I felt attracted to you the first time I saw you and I'm ashamed to tell you how I felt when we were on my bike."

I laugh out loud.

"How did you feel? Linc"

"Err, good would be the descriptive word."

We both laugh as I look at my watch.

"It's getting a little late Linc do you mind if we head home? My workload tomorrow is pretty grand."

We stand up and leave the restaurant paying our bill on the way out.

"How old are you Linc?"

He looks at me in surprise.

"Boy, you come straight to the point don't you? I'm 42."

"When is your birthday?"

"April. Are you going to tell me why you're asking?"

"Just curious Linc, I had guessed you to be between 35 and 40."

"Well thank you, now that's a compliment. I have guessed *you* to be 22."

"Very good, I am 22 I'll be 23 in November. You know Linc, it does not matter to me that you are 42; I've always been more attracted to older men. I've analyzed myself and come up with the conclusion that I prefer older men because I'm close to my father."

"Lucky me." He says.

We laugh again. I have noticed that I laugh a lot around Linc, which is definitely a good thing. We arrive back at my place 30 minutes later.

"I really like you Sydney, there is no point pretending besides it's quite obvious. At my age one tends to know what one wants and you also know it when you meet a special woman. There are a couple of things about myself that I need to tell you but that's for another day. Right now I just want to let you know that I have already started to care for you and I'd like to see you on a regular basis."

I am a bit overwhelmed. I really like Linc too; maybe this relationship *will* turn out very well. Maybe we'll get serious, well in a way it will be serious because I have no intention of dating more than one person at a time.

"I'm flattered Professor." I say smiling." I want to see you too."

He takes a step closer to me and holds out his arms. I move toward him and he gathers me in his arms in a big hug. I let myself relax in his arms and enjoy his embrace. I'm happy, I am in the company of a man that I'd only met three weeks ago but with whom I feel totally at ease. A sense of calm came over me; it feels almost as if Linc is my big brother, my protector, my confidant as well as the new man in my life. As I smile and pull back from Linc, still holding his hands, I wonder what Dad is going to say, I already know Mama's opinion. I guess I'll wait a while before I tell him. Linc also has to leave so we say our good nights and he kisses me on the cheek as I walk him to the door. I settle down on my couch and pick up the phone. I'm excited. With a smile on my face I started dialing Tiffany's number in Madrid, Spain; I have some great news for my friend!

CHAPTER 12
LINCOLN CALDWELL

Friday May 12th
Manhattan, NY

"Hello."

"Hiya Linc, are you asleep?"

"Not quite, Sydney, I was sure *you* would be though."

"I know I'm sorry. I just got off the phone with Tiffany, a friend of mine in Spain. We've been talking for the last 2 hours. I just brought her up to date on my New York experiences, including you."

I laugh.

"I just want to hear your voice again Linc, that's the real reason I'm calling."

"I've been thinking about you too. I was beginning to drop off to sleep but now that you've called I'm wide-awake. Maybe I should come over there so that I can give you another hug."

"Hmmm, don't tempt me Linc. It's already after midnight; by the time you get here all I'll want to do is cuddle up in your arms and sleep."

Sydney and I end up talking into the early hours of the morning. At 3.20a.m we finally say good night, after telling each other we'll speak later on in the day. I have more or less told her my life story also. I told her about my being a Georgia boy, my being an orphan since I was 20 and that I have a younger sister in Germany who is an army Captain. I told her how much I love my art and my lecturing. The two of us really have a lot in common and we could see that there is good chance our relationship could work. She also told me about her mother being apprehensive of our dating. I had told Sydney that I could understand her mother's concern but I would put her mother's mind at ease as time went by. She had also questioned me regarding sex before marriage again. As far as I was concerned it would not be a problem for me, *I hope*! At least that's what I have told Sydney. Of course I've let her know it isn't going to be the easiest thing in the world to do! We had laughed and joked about it, both of us realizing the seriousness of the topic.

I thought about the entire gang giving me encouraging thumbs up regarding Sydney. Carla and Ryoko in particular were so enthusiastic that they had both asked me to keep them abreast of developments in the relationship. The only person to voice any slight concerns had been Woody but everyone else including his wife Lola had descended on him like a ton of bricks! Woody's concern is the same as Valerie's, Sydney's and my age difference! He believes that 20 years is way too much. There's only a three-year gap between him and Lola, 45 and 42. He feels that in latter years the age gap will begin to show.

"You guys are from two different generations." Woody had said.

"What will happen when you're 60 Linc and Sydney is only 40? A 40 year old woman is still vibrant, what about children? If say the two of you have a child when you're 44 and she's 24 it means when that child is 16 you'll already be 60. Remember *I* should know what I'm talking about. I'm 45 now and we still don't have a child yet. "

I didn't even get a chance to respond because Ryoko, Ricky, Carla and Lola had all jumped down Woody's throat in my defense. Eventually Woody agreed to disagree with all of us, saying he was only looking out for my best interests and for me to proceed with caution. Everything considered it was very good feedback and I feel glad that my friends are pleased with my choice. Not that the gang determined who I should date but it is a good sign for me. We have all spent so much time together over the past three or four years that we all respect one another's opinion.

I look at the bedside clock 4.15a.m; I need to get some sleep. I make sure my alarm is set to the right time and close my eyes.

CHAPTER 13
SYDNEY COLLINS

Sunday 22nd October
Salou, Spain

"Two thousand Pesetas, two thousand Pesetas" the peddler repeats

"Honey don't you think that's a little too expensive for that carving? After all it's only 3 inches tall" I ask Linc.

"Yep, I think so too. Let's haggle a bit more." He replies.

We are walking along the beach in Salou, Spain. It is beautiful, it is serene, the seawater is crystal clear and the palm trees and coconut trees are picturesque. The breeze is also perfect, not too strong; just enough to tussle my hair and lift my sun dress a couple of inches. As far as the eye can see there are waves tipped with foam washing ashore in a gentle flow. A couple of people are horseback riding along the shore, the waves lapping the horses' hooves. Linc and I had driven down here from Tarragona just 30 minutes up the highway to spend the day. We had arrived in Salou at 10.30a.m this morning and walked up and down bare-foot on the white sands of the beach. We have also visited every shop that lined the road that ran along-side the beach. There are restaurants, a couple of small banks, food stalls and clothes shops and other shops and stalls selling everything from small pieces of furniture to carvings and ceremonial masks, swords and knives. We've bought a few carvings and some rugs. Linc has also purchased a painting of two matadors in a bullring, which he adores. My favorite purchase so far is a 10inch ballerina dressed in a beautiful red, gold and black traditional costume. She is holding a tambourine with her hands above her head and she is twirling with her full skirt billowing out. It is lovely. On a street running parallel behind the shops are a dozen hotels, some large and some very small. Linc and I have been in Spain for the past one week. We had taken a 90-minute train ride from Barcelona to Tarragona early this morning and rented a car to come to Salou. It had been interesting to notice that most of the residents of Salou spoke Catalan and not Spanish.

Our visit here in Spain has so far turned out to be the best vacation I'd ever taken. The people are all friendly; their friendliness had been the same in Barcelona and in Madrid. Tiffany had met us at the airport in Barcelona a week ago. She had moved from Madrid to Barcelona in August after completing her 3month training. She has accepted a 2year contract with the same company and has settled down nicely.
"You know Sydney; I could live the rest of my life here in Spain." She had told me.
I can see what she means; I have fallen in love with Spain too!

After spending two days in Barcelona (I had stayed with Tiffany at her house while Linc had stayed at a hotel), we had taken a long train journey to Madrid. The Barcelona to Madrid trip had taken about 8 hours but it had allowed us to see the Spanish countryside. We had found a hotel in downtown Madrid to spend the night. Linc had been great and not given me any stress about our separate rooms. In fact over the past five months since we've been dating, he has been wonderful about not giving me any undue sexual pressure. The last five months have also been great. I've fallen completely in love with Linc and he has made me very happy. Almost everything about him makes me tingle inside and it has sometimes been a struggle even for me, regarding the 'abstinence' issue. Anyway we had walked a lot through downtown Madrid; at some local jewelers I had been able to buy the best priced 18 carat gold jewelry ever! We had also watched a blockbuster movie translated into Spanish, just for the fun of it.

It's nearly 6p.m as we head back to Tarragona to catch the train to Barcelona. One of the sights that caught my eye the most in Tarragona was an ancient Roman Amphitheater. We had actually taken a few minutes to join other tourists in walking amongst the ruins. We saw dilapidated dungeons and the remnants of slave chains and shackles still attached to the broken walls. Now on the train back to Barcelona I again reminisce about the previous five months of my relationship with Linc. The only snag so far has been Mama's continuous dislike of our dating. She has nothing against Linc as a person; it's just our age difference that she can't deal with. Omar of course is also against it but I'm not concerned about him. Dad surprisingly is rather non-committal; he just keeps telling me that he likes Linc too and since he obviously makes me happy, then he's happy for me. I'm not sure whether this is a good sign or a bad sign from Dad. But the longer I think about it I remember, that if Dad is against it, he'd have let me know in no uncertain terms. I think about the couple of times I have snuck away from work and hopped on the subway to meet Linc on campus. Fordham University in the Bronx, from CSD, is only 20 minutes by train. CSD is now fully operational and has been for the past 3 months. We have a full staff of 20 persons including Adam Whittaker and myself. I've also found a church I like and I have been attending Sunday services as often as I can.

"Will you talk to me when you're through day dreaming?"

"Don't you think I've been talking your ears off all day?" I chuckle.

"Have I complained yet? I can listen to you all day long, you know that honey." Linc adds, laughing.

"Uh huh, I thought you Georgia boys liked silent girls."

"Not me, are you sure you can't sing too?"

"Linc if you don't quit teasing me about my singing I'm going to team up with Ryoko and we're going to kick your behind."

"Sure, I just haven't told you I've been taking secret Kung Fu lessons. When I went on that three-week trip to the Tibetan monastery *that* is all I did."

"What Tibetan monastery? Being professor of creative writing has certainly fired up your imagination."

"Anyway, it's true I can't sing but I can at least write poetry. Can't I?" I ask

"Yes you certainly can. Thanks again for the poem you wrote me yesterday 'Roses are always red'. I've got it folded in my wallet."

"Very sweet of you sir, it seems I will not need Ryoko's services after all."

Mentioning Ryoko's name reminds me again of that first night Linc had told me of their 4-year relationship. I have no problem with the fact that they are such good friends even now and I definitely like her. It is just that sometimes I get a little pang when I see them together. I too am now used to calling Lola and Woody, Ricky, Ryoko and Carla 'the gang'. All of us have been out a few times and I've enjoyed their company. I also know that Woody has reservations about Linc and I. Funny enough Ryoko and Carla are my favorites. I've been to see Carla perform at the 'Cotton Club' twice and she's still as hilarious as ever.

I snuggle up closer to Linc and close my eyes in an attempt to sleep but he's in a playful mood.
"Hey wake up." he says.
He starts tickling me, which always drives me crazy.
"Stop, stop, honey please! I'm going to scream. Aaahhh! Stop everybody's looking at us."
"Tell me how much you love me again." He says grinning.
"Okay, okay but I protest. I'm under duress it's not fair. Aaahhh, stop… okay I love you, I love you, I love you!"
"That's better sweetheart….I love you too, very much!"
He put his arm around me and I finally fall asleep smiling.

CHAPTER 14
SYDNEY COLLINS

Friday 27th October
Manhattan, NY

Linc and I had gone to the airport by taxi. Tiffany had said her goodbyes to us early in the morning on her way to work. Linc had spent the last night in Barcelona with us at Tiffany's house and we'd all talked practically all night Monday. Eventually he had fallen asleep on the sofa and Tiffany and I had gone upstairs to bed. Our flight from Barcelona to New York had been late Tuesday morning and we had arrived back in New York rather tired but ready for a proper meal. The time difference put us into JFK early afternoon local time. The past three days at work have been very busy. Even Adam had been swamped with the workload and it had taken all of three days to catch up.

The phone rings interrupting my thoughts,
"Good morning, CSD, this is Sydney, how may I help you?"
"Hello Sydney, this is Carla. I thought I'd give you a quick call to welcome you back home. Sorry I haven't been able to speak to you since Tuesday, I've just got back from Florida last night."
"Thanks Carla how was your trip?"
"No, no, no girl. You tell me about Spain. I want all the nitty gritty and any dirty secrets as well." she says laughing.
I laugh too. Carla is being her inquisitive, naughty and funny self.
"We had a wonderful time Carla; I'll give you the details later, how about meeting up this evening?"
"Great, good idea, where do you want to meet?"
There is a knock on my office door.
"Hold on, just one minute please Carla, my secretary has just walked into my office carrying a large bouquet of flowers and a box of chocolates."

"Miss Collins, these flowers and chocolates were just delivered for you." Liz, my secretary told me.

"Thank you Liz, please put them right here."

"Carla? I'm reading the card on the flowers; you won't believe who sent them." I say in an annoyed tone.

"What's wrong Sydney? Who sent them, you sound upset?"

"I'm *very* upset Carla. Omar sent them! He's also put in the note that he's coming to New York next week and that I should pick him up at La Guardia. As soon as I've finished speaking with you, I'm going to call him in LA and chew him out. He knows better. Linc and I have been seeing each other for five months now. I really think he should leave me alone."

"Relax honey. The man just isn't ready to give up yet. I remember all the stuff you told me about him. He's been at IBM in LA for the past five months and probably feels that he hasn't met anyone else like you out there. When you do call him try to be nice okay? But be firm." Carla says.

"Firm yes, nice I can't promise. Don't you think it's rather disrespectful Carla? After all, we've had that conversation a dozen times over the past few months and I've told Omar that I love Linc and nobody is taking me away from him."

"Well at least you've got two men wanting you. I haven't got any do you want to give me one of yours?" Carla laughs.

I had to laugh too. Carla is just too much!

"Okay Carla, I'll try to be nice but I will tell him not to come to New York and if he insists that he's coming then I'm certainly not picking him up at the airport. Fair enough?"

"Fair enough, you go girl." She laughs again.

"Oh guess what Carla."

"What."

"The chocolates are 'Cadbury's Milk Tray', my favorite."

"My favorites too honey. If you don't know what to do with them, send them to me."

"Carla, I love you, crazy woman." I chuckle. "I'll probably do just that. I'll call you after 3pm okay?"

"Okay hon, speak to you later. Bye!"

Just as Carla hangs up; the phone rings again and Adam also walks into my office.

"Hi Adam. This call is either Linc or one of my parents, please give me a second."

"Of course Sydney, go right ahead, I'll come back in a few minutes."

"Hello, CSD, Sydney speaking."

"Hello sweetheart. I love it when you answer the phone like that, on your private line even when you know it's a personal call."

"Hi Dad, I've got to be a consummate professional at work. Don't you agree?"

"Uh huh, I certainly do. Just as I've always said, CSD is in good hands."

"Thank you Dad. How is Ma?"

"She's fine. I just called to let you know that we'll be coming to New York on Monday. It's just a day trip. We'll be leaving in the evening. Could you ask Adam to call me? I'd like him to meet me at the airport. There are a couple of issues I'd like to discuss with him in the car en-route to the office."

"Okay Dad, Adam was actually here with me a few seconds ago. By the way Dad, Omar says he's coming to New York next week and he wants me to meet him at La Guardia. He also sent me a large bouquet of flowers and a box of chocolates. What is wrong with him? I've told him that we can only be friends and nothing more. I wish he would leave me alone."

"Hmmm, that's odd. He's been speaking with your mother frequently over the past couple of weeks, while you were in Spain. Maybe she knows about his intended trip to New York. She hasn't mentioned anything to me though."

"Dad! I hope Mama isn't encouraging Omar. Is Mama there? I'd like to speak to her."

"She's right here sweetheart, hold on."

"Hello Sydney."

"Hello Ma. Ma do you know Omar wants to come and see me in New York next week?"

"Yes I do. He told me a couple of days ago."

"Why? Did you discourage him?"

"Of course not! Don't be silly. Omar can go wherever he pleases; it's a free country is it not?"

"Mama please don't encourage him. You know how I feel about Linc. I know that you don't approve but you *do* like Linc also. I'm going to call Omar in a few minutes to give him a piece of my mind in no uncertain terms either."

"Be civil young lady. Omar hasn't done anything wrong."

"Yes he has Mama. He's constantly trying to break me and Linc up. That's uncalled for and disrespectful to both Linc and me. Every conversation Omar has with me ends with him saying something rude or unwelcome about Linc. I've had enough of it."

"Well, you do what you feel is necessary and maybe I will too."

"Can I speak to Dad please?" I ask.

"Dad, why is Mama doing this?"

"Don't worry too much sweetheart. I'll speak to her. I'll sort it out okay? Take it easy. Give me a call later this evening I've got to go now. Love you. Bye sweetheart."

"Bye Dad. I love you too."

This last conversation had drained me emotionally a little. Mama has decided to be difficult and to continue to encourage Omar. It looks like Linc and I have a battle on our hands where Mama is concerned. Omar is not a problem I can handle him. So far Linc has been the perfect gentleman I'm just a little concerned about if Linc's or Omar's egos get in the way. Maybe the best thing to do for now is to immerse myself in work! I pass Dad's message on to Adam and got on with my office responsibilities.

At 5.10p.m I call Carla and we agree to meet at my place. I tell her about my conversation with my parents and she is understandably worried. After she promises to make it as quickly as possible I hang up, gather my papers and briefcase and head for home.

CHAPTER 15
SYDNEY COLLINS

Monday 30th October
New York, NY

"They should be landing in a few minutes." Adam remarks.

"I hope so. We've been here 30minutes already. I can imagine Dad will be frustrated, he hates it when flights are delayed at the last minute."

"Same here Sydney, especially if you're informed about it only after you've already boarded the plane."

While Adam and I wait for my parents' plane to land I smile as I remember my weekend. I had spent a very relaxing couple of days with Linc even though we'd gone out to a couple of places on Saturday. Friday evening with Carla had also been relaxing, she and I had played a couple of games of chess and she had cooked me a fabulous dinner. We'd had such a good time that I convinced her to spend the night. On Saturday Linc and I had gone to the Empire State building, taken the ferry across the Hudson River and spent the rest of the weekend chilling in front of the television, except for Sunday when we'd gone to my church. Linc even got to meet my Pastor. I was glad he had finally agreed to come to my church but I know he is still a long way from giving his life to Christ. Although Linc attended the Methodist church near his apartment about once or twice a month, he still thinks that any Minister of the gospel, less than 50 years old, doesn't know what he's talking about! Linc feels that living your life in a 'good' way is the ticket to heaven. I've tried to explain the difference between his school of thought and what Jesus preached. I've made references to Jesus' teachings on the only way to heaven is to believe in your heart that he is Lord and also confess it with your mouth! I've told him that the bible says that we are 'saved by grace and not by works lest any man should boast'. Over the past

17 to 18 months I've often wondered whether the older generation found it more difficult to come to Jesus because of the doctrine they'd been brought up on. Dad and Mama's views on what they term 'this new wave of Christianity' are similar to Linc's. Well at least Linc has taken the first step, which was coming with me to *my* church rather than going to his. He has also listened to one or two of the taped sermons I had given him.

I had spoken to Omar on Friday and it hadn't been a pleasant conversation at all. The long and short of it is he's no longer coming to see me in New York. He probably will not call me for a long time either. I feel both relief and sadness. Omar and I, up till when I came to New York had really been good friends. I have tolerated his overtures and sometimes they had been overly bothersome. During the entire period we've known each other the two things we argue about constantly are sex and religion. As I've mentioned earlier Omar is Agnostic, he believes entirely in his own efforts and that if there is a God, He (God) has nothing to do with whether or not he (Omar) succeeds in life. He does not believe God blesses people with individual talents.

The past 5 months with Linc have shown me that a woman can have a loving relationship with a man and not have sexual intercourse with him.

"You look like you're deep in thought Sydney."
"I am Adam. I was just remembering my conversation with Omar. It didn't go down well but I think all's well that ends well, at least in this particular case."
"I hope so Sydney." Adam replies.

A few minutes later my parents' plane lands. As expected, Dad is not in a good mood. Mama had taken the brunt of Dad's irritation during the flight from Boston. Because I want to speak with Mama, I get into a cab with her while Adam and Dad go in the car.

"Ma, I've spoken with Omar and he's no longer coming to New York to see me. Of course we argued and disagreed but my mind is made up and I will not be civil to him even if he does show up."

After a short pause I realize Mama has decided to give me the silent treatment. I am upset with Mama also, so I decide that I'm not going to say anything else either. The cab ride to the office takes approximately 40 minutes and throughout that time Mama did not say a word! During the course of the day I got to tell Dad about my conversation with Omar and my non-conversation with Mama.

"I did speak with your mother sweetheart, more than once to be exact. She has more or less resigned herself to accepting it but she's not going to ease up on you."

"Thanks Dad, I'm prepared for that."

My parents left on a late night flight and I got home very tired. I call Linc and tell him about my day.

"Hi honey."

"Hi Sydney, I've missed you all day today."

"Really? I bet you say that to all the girls."

"Of course I do. That's why I'm the most eligible bachelor in the city." Linc says chuckling.

"Are you sure about that? I met a girl just yesterday who doesn't know who you are." I tease.

"She must have been an out-of-towner or a foreigner."

"Hmmm, maybe you're right." I laugh.

I go on to tell Linc about today and as usual he takes it in his stride.

"Just give her some more time honey." He says. "I'm sure she'll come around."

"I really hope so. I've been praying for it for a while. I know God will answer my prayers I just hope it'll be soon." I add.

"Didn't you tell me that God is not a God of confusion?"

"Yes."

"Well then, I'm sure your prayers will be answered soon."

Linc and I talk for another 10 minutes or so before I beg off. I'm so sleepy that I am beginning to fall asleep while talking.

Suddenly the phone rings, waking me up. I look at my bedside clock…12.33a.m! Who could this be? Is it Linc calling me back? I pick up the phone.

"Hello." I answer, sleepily.

"Wake up stranger you're on conference-call. Guess who this is."

"…Khreeo? Is that you?"

"Yes it is and there is someone-else on the line too."

"Hi Sydney, it's Kephern. How are you girlfriend?"

"Kephern! Khreeo! You two crazy people, where have you guys been?" I exclaim. "Where are you guys calling from?"

"I'm in Boston; I just came home from LA yesterday." Khreeo says.

"And I'm in Seattle, Sydney. We're sorry we haven't called sooner but since we both got back from Mexico last month, settling down has been tough for the both of us. Especially with me being in Seattle and my baby in LA." Kephern complains.

"Mexico! When did you guys go to Mexico? I thought after graduation you were both going to Seattle."

"That *was* the plan but Khreeo's job fell through. So we took a vacation, a long one. We were in Mexico for about 4 months. We might not even have come back now, but I got a very lucrative job offer with an accounting firm here in Seattle." Kephern continues.

"Khreeo just got a job in LA last week and she decided to take it. In fact it's because she ran into Omar that we were able to get your number."

"So how have you been doing Sydney?" Khreeo asks.

"Great, Khreeo. I've got a million and one things to tell you and Kephern. There is a very special man in my life."

"So we hear girl! Omar gave me the lowdown or should I say he gave me an earful. So who is this lucky guy?" Khreeo asks.

"His name is Lincoln Caldwell. He's a professor of creative writing and an artist." I answer.

"To tell you the truth Sydney, Omar didn't have anything nice to say about the man." Kephern confides.

"Omar is …he hasn't even met Linc. I've told him never to call me again. He's made me wonder what I ever saw in him. I can't believe

Omar's jealousy has caused him to act and talk so immaturely! Guys, let's please not mention Omar right now okay? You'll get a chance to meet Linc soon and you'll see for yourselves."

"You're right Sydney. Let's talk about something else, like when are we going to see you again?" Khreeo probes.

"I don't know. Are you guys coming to New York soon?" I reply.

"Maybe. Tell you what Sydney. It's pretty late over there on the east coast so how about if we call you later on in the week?" Kephern concludes.

"Okay guys I'll be looking out for your call. Let me give you the office number and Kephern, please give me your number in Seattle too."

Kephern, Khreeo and I update our phone numbers and after promising to call again we all hang up. I'm pleasantly surprised at their call. They are my other two friends from college and I hadn't spoken to them in 6 months! Now that they have contacted me we'll certainly be speaking to one another regularly. I get out of bed and get a drink of water then I go back to bed and fall asleep almost immediately.

CHAPTER 16
LINCOLN CALDWELL

Wednesday November 14th
Manhattan, NY

Life has been good lately, especially since I'd met Sydney. I've had 6 months of bliss and I'm looking forward to many more years of it. I have a surprise planned for Sydney tomorrow. Tomorrow is her birthday and I'm going to propose to her. Ryoko had by clandestine methods, been able to obtain Sydney's ring size for me. The only other person who knows about the surprise is Carla and that's because she's also involved in the arrangements. I'll be taking Sydney to the Southside Seaport in the morning, we'll visit the shops and the restaurants and she'll also be able to sit and view both the East River and the Hudson River. She has been urging me to take her to the Seaport for at least two weeks but I've been too busy. Then later in the evening the whole gang will be meeting up at the 'Cotton Club'. I intend to propose to Sydney by getting on stage in front of the entire audience. Hopefully she'll say YES!

    I feel like the luckiest man on earth. I have four very good friends, one of whom is genuinely happy for me in my relationship with Sydney even though she herself is a former girlfriend. Four years together wasn't anything to sneeze at and so I know that I will always have a sort of special place in my heart for Ryoko. Especially due to the way she has welcomed Sydney. To top everything off I feel blessed that Sydney and I are so much in love.

    Time to concentrate on my work. I've given my students an exam and I am only halfway through marking and grading their papers. If I spend all day and this evening, I should be able to complete them.

The stage is set; today has been perfect so far. Sydney and I have taken the subway to the Seaport. I had met her at home at 10a.m this morning with a huge bunch of assorted roses and 30 minutes later we had strolled to the nearest subway station. By 4.30p.m we had visited the mall located along the edge of the water and bought a few items from the souvenir shops. I have also bought a couple of tee shirts for the two teenage children of one of my professor colleagues at Fordham. Dr. Tendai Mugweni is on vacation from Harare, Zimbabwe with his two sons. In addition Sydney and I have viewed Ellis Island and the statue of Liberty from the ferry we had taken around Manhattan. Of course we saw both the East River and the Hudson River and had even taken a quick walk along Wall Street.

Today's outing has somehow reminded me of our trip to Spain. Maybe it's being out and about or holding hands sightseeing. I really can't put my finger on it but whatever it is, I like it. I remember Barcelona and the city's 1.6 million residents who actually make up one 6th of Spain's entire population! Sydney and I had probably had most of our fun in Barcelona. We had watched a game of Castells. A game that had originated in Catalan and consists of 100 people or more climbing on top of one another to heights of 35 feet or more. Needless to say all the participants got insured before the game. We had also strolled along the Las Ramblas, a tree-lined boulevard with a wide center walkway, which the Spanish locals claim to be the world's best pedestrian promenade! Las Ramblas actually extends all the way from the port to the city center. The architecture in both Barcelona and Madrid city centers is incredible. We visited famous landmarks like the Gothic Catedral de Barcelona where each Sunday natives perform a Catalonian folk dance that had once been forbidden by Fransisco Franco, a former King of Spain. I recall how excited Sydney had been when we saw the 1992 Olympic stadium. She had told me that this stadium had been considered the best in the world prior to the recent extravaganza in Sydney, Australia! The Paseo de Gracia Avenue and the Sagrada Familia church created by Gaudi a famous Spanish architect, were also another two exciting places Sydney and I had seen in Barcelona. All in all Spain had been 100%

perfect for us. The people, the sites, the food, the scenery and the general atmosphere of Spain had been intoxicating. To say that we had thoroughly enjoyed ourselves was an understatement! We would certainly be going back to Spain someday soon, I'm hoping. Sydney and I both enjoy traveling but we also feel that we should see more of the United States as well.

Well we're home now and tomorrow I'm about to ask this lovely woman to be my wife. If all goes well I shall be the happiest man in New York by nightfall.

CHAPTER 17
SYDNEY COLLINS-CALDWELL

Friday, 15ᵗʰ November----2 Years Later
Manhattan, NY

I wish it would stop raining, it's nearly 7pm and it's been wet all day long. Normally I don't mind the rain but lately I've been irritable and restless. I'd wanted to go out today but I wasn't in the mood to deal with this downpour. Besides, today is my birthday and I feel as if I could use some cheering up. Linc should be home soon and maybe he has a surprise for me, actually I'm sure he has. He has been such a wonderful husband, friend, mentor and lover! Hmm, that last adjective brought a smile to my face. It has been two years of marital bliss for me. We had gotten married 19months ago and here I am, propped up in an armchair with my swollen feet up on an ottoman and 6 months pregnant! Yep, that's right, 6 months pregnant! The pregnancy part was inevitable the way Linc and I made love, everywhere in the home at anytime of the day or night. We both agreed that we were making up for lost time. He has turned out to be all I could ever ask for in a husband and I feel like the luckiest woman alive.

Our wedding ceremony hadn't been a very large one on my insistence. Left to Dad there would have been at least 500 guests but he'd had to settle for only 50. My family, mum and dad, Linc's sister Lynn (flew in from Germany), my friends Kephern, Khreeo, Tiffany and of course 'the gang' Woody, Lola, Ricky, Ryoko had all been there. Adam Whittaker and a few other CSD co-workers had also flown in for the wedding, which had taken place in April last year in Boston, and it had been grand! The ceremony itself was rather musical. Linc had secretly arranged for two saxophone players to play a few of my jazz and R&B favorites, like George Benson's 'Greatest Love of All', Anita Baker's 'Sweet Love', Grover Washington's 'Just the Two of Us', Kenny G/ Peabo Bryson's 'By The Time This Night Is Over' and Barry White's 'Walking In The Rain With The One I Love'. My wedding dress was very simple but elegant, it is white (I still have the dress of course), and it has beads and sequins on it. Mama had objected to the white wedding dress because she hadn't believed I was still a virgin and that nobody else would either. Mama had also objected to the marriage itself. She still feels that I shouldn't have married Linc, mainly because of our age difference. It didn't seem to matter to her that Linc makes me very happy or that she herself is more than just a few years younger than Dad. Anyway I had decided that on my wedding day I was going to be happy and nothing was going to spoil that day for me.

Instead of driving off in the limousine after the service, we had ridden off on Linc's new dressed up Harley Davidson Soft-Tail motorcycle. We only rode the bike half a mile though, just to where the limo had been waiting. But it had certainly been a sight to see, me in my wedding dress, Linc in his tuxedo, hopping onto the bike and the guests looking shocked and unbelieving. Linc had planned for the Limo driver to drive off just as we were coming out of the church, so that people would wonder what was going on. They could see the Limo leaving without the bride and groom in it. That, of course had some people shouting and running after the limo trying to catch the driver's attention. Linc and I had stood there laughing for a minute or so and then Ricky had wheeled out the Harley from behind a parked van! The three of us (Linc, Ricky and I) had almost fallen over from laughing at most peoples' expressions, especially Ma's. Of course Mama had told me a couple of months later that we had been irresponsible.

Mama of course is still her old self. She doesn't like Linc any less but also hasn't warmed to him either. Since Linc and I have been married Mama has visited us only once. We speak with her and Dad on the phone quite regularly but even the phone conversations have dwindled because everyone has been so busy. I've missed work more than a couple of days recently due to my nausea. The 1st trimester of my pregnancy has been quite trying for me. I have thrown up a lot. On two separate occasions I have vomited into my office trash bin before I could make it to the ladies room. Of course Adam and my other staff had promptly sent me home and called Linc at work to inform him of my embarrassing drama. Both Carla and Ryoko have been very supportive and have been frequent visitors at home. Subsequently, I've eaten a lot of spicy Japanese cooking lately and it's been very good. I haven't been able to eat breakfast because anything I eat has to be spicy in order to suppress the nausea. My eating habits have therefore changed and I haven't really gained much weight at all in my pregnancy. My doctor has been a little concerned about my weight, especially since during my most recent sonogram we found out that I was carrying twins! Both Linc and I are doubly excited over this news and so the February 25th due date can't arrive soon enough for us. We've both decided that we don't want to know the sex of the babies until they're born. Although we both want identical twins of the same sex I would prefer a set of girls. Linc on the other hand doesn't seem to mind either way.

"Where is Linc anyway?" I say out loud.

"He should be home by now. It's 7:15pm; I'll call him on his cell phone." I continue, still talking to myself.

I pick up the cordless handset and stretch lazily and got up from the armchair. I wander over to the kitchen intending to pour myself a glass of orange juice. Just then the doorbell rings. Who could that be? I wonder. It couldn't be Linc he's got his own keys. I direct my protruding belly toward the front door. I peek through the spy-hole but can only see a bunch of flowers and not who is holding them. This is probably Linc trying to surprise me, I think to myself.

"Who is it?" I ask.

I could hear more than one voice chuckling from behind the door but no one answers me.

"Well whoever it is I'd like to warn you that there are three of us about to open this door, so beware." I continue, laughing as I speak.

I open the door and am utterly and excitedly surprised to find Linc, Dad, Kephern, Khreeo, Lynn, Ricky, Ryoko, Carla, Woody and Lola all huddling together at the doorway, all trying to catch my initial surprised reaction. I jump up and hug Linc and then Dad, all the while giggling and laughing and trying to talk at the same time.

"How did you do this Linc? How did you get everyone here at the same time? Dad, when did you get into town? Oh, this is so great. I love you all. Linc, you're a sweetheart I need this, I've been brooding all day long, I love you!" I gush out. Everyone continues laughing as we crowd into the living room and I continue hugging and kissing everyone.

"Khreeo and Kephern I can't believe it. Don't tell me you guys have finally agreed to move to New York, have you?"

"Uh uh Sydney. Remember we don't like cold weather. When we move from Seattle we're going south toward the equator, okay." Kephern replies.

"Besides, you and Linc have mentioned the possibility of moving too. So there wouldn't be anyone here for us anyway." Khreeo adds.

""Hey, what about *us* lovely people?" Ryoko chides.

"Yeah, the rest of us are still a wonderful group aren't we honey?" Woody asks his wife.

"Right you are Woody" Lola answers.

"Maybe Kephern is just afraid that some New York wolf will snatch Khreeo up. Come on Kephern, you can confide in us. We promise not to put it out in the New York Times 'Seattle man afraid his beautiful girlfriend will run off with Yankee doodle-do" Ricky said laughing loudly.

Everyone laughs, including Kephern, which was a good thing because Kephern had been a little wary of Ricky ever since Linc and I got married. He had been upset on our wedding day that she had spent too much time laughing, talking and dancing with Ricky. I had noticed too but hadn't thought much of it until Khreeo had confided in me, on more than one occasion in fact, that she's a little disillusioned with Kephern. Mainly because he still hasn't asked her to marry him, even though they've been seeing each other for over 5 years and both families have been expecting it. Khreeo now at 26, has been ready for a couple of years and has begun to feel that maybe she's wasting her time with Kephern, who on the other hand says he's in no rush to get married, especially since he's 'only' 26 also and 50% of all marriages end in divorce anyway.

"Well sweetheart, how are you feeling now?" Dad asks.

"Much, much better now that you all are here" I reply.

"How did you all fit into the elevator?" I continue.

"We didn't. Lynn, Ricky, Dad and I came up the stairs," Linc said.

"And I made it up faster than these two young bucks too!" Dad adds, laughing and pointing at Linc and Ricky. I gave Dad another hug and kiss.

"I hope you like your flowers and candy. Sorry they're not 'Cadbury's milk tray' but I'm sure you'll find them to be real good. Believe me; I've tried them a few times myself." Carla chirps in, with a big smile on her face.

"I'm sure I will Carla, thanks."

I have a lot of flowers. Linc had brought in a huge bunch. Carla, Lynn and Dad had also brought smaller bunches which were just as beautiful.

"Linc honey, can you help me with these flowers please" I ask.

"Sure thing Sydney" he replies.

"I'll help you too Sydney" Khreeo says as she walks with Linc and I to the kitchen.

I guess she wants to talk and I'm right. As soon as we are out of earshot she starts.

"You know guys I really think Kephern and I are on our last legs together. I've run out of patience with him"

"Hmmm. Every story has two sides, maybe he's feeling pressured. Look at me, I was over 40 when we got married" Linc says.

"Yes but you hadn't been dating Sydney for 5 years had you? And when you did meet her it only took you what? Less than 6 months to ask her?"

"I agree Khreeo but at 26 I wasn't ready either. Maybe Kephern will be ready next month. Who knows?" Linc answers.

"Too much uncertainty for me."

"It seems you've already make up your mind Khreeo" I inject.

"I love both you guys so how about we talk about this a little later. Remember it's my birthday and I don't want to get depressed again thinking about you two splitting up. Okay?"

"You're right Sydney. I'm sorry," she says, hugging me.

A few moments later as we continue with putting the flowers into fresh water, Lynn comes and joins us in the kitchen.

"Hey, what's up in here? I thought I'd join the birthday girl and big brother," she says.

Lynn had concluded her tour of duty in the army and had returned from Germany nearly a year ago. She's settled down in Roswell, Georgia, on the outskirts of Atlanta. I really like her. Apart from the fact that she's Linc's only sister, I feel as if I have become friends with her too. She's a lot like Linc. They are both quietly strong personalities, both have artistic gifts. Lynn only paints for fun though, which means maybe one or two paintings in 3 years but from her unfinished work upstairs in the gallery, it is very good. Physically they are also similar. Lynn is my height 5ft. 10ins, with an athletic build. At around 35 years old she looks like she could still run track competitively. Someone, I can't recall whom, a couple of years ago had commented that Linc and I looked a little alike. More recently at a movie theatre, the ticket attendant had told Linc and I the same thing. When we mentioned that we were married the attendant had remarked that his mum and dad had started to look alike to him too! In my opinion though it is Lynn and I that bear a resemblance to one another. So much so that both of us had noticed it but surprisingly enough Linc could not see it.

"Hi Lynn. It's good of you to come, I suppose turning 25 requires family and friends around" I say.

"Yep, I can't remember when *I* turned twenty-five though, it's been sooo long ago" Lynn laughs.

"Really? Well you certainly don't look like you're a day older than twenty-five still, Sis." Linc comments.

"Thanks big brother."

"I think it's time for other important things." Ricky says, also walking into the kitchen.

"What's for dinner?" He adds, opening up the refrigerator and the oven doors at the same time.

"Oh no! I…er…wasn't expecting company so I only made enough dinner as usual." I stammer.

Linc, Khreeo, Lynn and Ricky burst out laughing.

"What's so funny?" I ask.

"Come over here sweetheart." Linc says, grabbing my hand.

He literally pulls me back to the living room with Khreeo, Lynn and Ricky in tow.

"Listen up everybody. Sydney is concerned about what we're all going to eat. Does anyone have any suggestions or ideas about aforementioned concerns?" Linc announces.

There are lots of murmurs and whispers and feigned ignorance and Ryoko is trying not to laugh.

Lola raises her hand and says, "How about we order pizza?"

"Pizza? You've got to be kidding. How can we eat pizza on Sydney's 25th birthday anniversary?" Woody scolds.

"I have a suggestion," Dad says.

"How about we all troop down to Sydney's favorite restaurant?"

"Good idea Dad I'd like to go to 'Dante's Steakhouse'. I feel like eating one of their steaks with some fresh salad," I say excitedly.

"Dante's it is then. Let's go everyone." Dad replies.

"What about reservations? There's only one Dante's in the whole of New York, how will we get in?" I inquire.

"Never mind Sydney, it's already been taken care of" Ryoko laughs.

"We all knew that you'd choose Dante's if given a choice so we'd made reservations since Monday"

"You guys are just too much. Is that when this surprise gathering was planned?"

"Well not quite. We had initially started…"

"Much earlier, actually 2 months ago to be exact!" Khreeo interrupts Kephern.

"It obviously took a lot of sneaking around on Linc's part to pull this off without arousing my suspicions." I smile.

"Okay people, I'm hungry. Can we go now?" Ricky moans from across the room.

"Oh be quiet Ricky! Where all the food you eat goes, no one knows anyway! It still looks like you can't weigh more than a buck and a half." Carla rejoins.

"I'll have you know young lady; I'm still a growing man. Besides there's a lot of lean muscle under this clothing and in my line of work I burn a lot of energy." Ricky replies with a wide grin.

CHAPTER 18
SYDNEY COLLINS-CALDWELL

Friday 15th November----continued
Manhattan, NY

Ten minutes later we are on our way. We end up in three different vehicles. Linc, Dad and I pile in with Carla into her Toyota Landcruiser, while Khreeo, Lynn and Ricky go in his car. That left Ryoko and Kephern to travel with Woody and Lola in their car. Of course Khreeo riding with Ricky doesn't go unnoticed by anyone and I feel a little uneasy about it. I can feel Kephern's agitation and I know trouble is brewing. Hopefully it won't all burst out tonight. Khreeo is in a playful mood but I don't feel that she should be flaunting any flirtations in Kephern's face. In my opinion he doesn't deserve it and besides I not sure whether Ricky (even at 40) is ready to settle down and get married yet. I smile ruefully as I think about the fact that my few best friends and I, all seem to prefer older men.

"What are you smiling about, what's on your mind Hon?"

Linc's voice breaks into my thoughts bringing me back to my immediate surroundings.

"It's *a woman's secret.*" I grin mischievously.

"No it's not; I bet you're going to tell me right now" Linc responds.

"There are no secrets between us and no hidden truths."

"Alright sweetheart, I am just thinking about Khreeo and Ricky. What do you think about the fact that Khreeo jumped into Ricky's car with him?"

"I don't know what to think Sydney; it seems to me that Khreeo is being a little naughty. She could have easily ridden with us or with Woody and Lola."

Dad has been silent for the past few minutes but decides to say something now.

"What are you guys worried about, if it turns out that Ricky and Khreeo like each other then so be it. You can't force these things you know. You two should know *exactly* what I'm talking about! " He says.

"Besides one of life's little goals should be to forget the failures of the past and embrace the promises of the future."

"*Dad*, you sound as if you have already doomed Khreeo and Kephern's relationship, there's a possibility that their relationship may still survive." I blurt out.

"I'm surprised at you Dad, what you said just now sounded rather negative, s*hame* on you!"

Carla, then Linc and Dad all start to laugh. For some reason everyone saw the humor in what I said but I couldn't. I have always assumed that those two would make it to the altar, just like Linc and I. The possibility that they may break up had not occurred to me and I'm not quite prepared. I suppose that there is a possible light at the end of the tunnel. After all if I were to choose someone for Khreeo, Ricky would be at the top of the list.

A couple of minutes later we pull up in front of 'Dante's'. Everyone gets out of the various cars and we walk into the restaurant as the valet attendants park the three vehicles.

I look at my wristwatch, *10:30 p.m*, I can't believe it, time has flown by so quickly. Something else that I can't believe is that I've eaten sooo... much! This must be the biggest meal I've eaten since I got pregnant. The evening had gone quite well. Everyone had thoroughly enjoyed their meal; the only hitch of the evening had been the altercation between Kephern, Khreeo and Ricky. Actually, the altercation had been a pretty bad one, so bad in fact, that Ricky and Kephern had practically come to blows! I couldn't believe it when it happened but Kephern had been a little bit upset all evening at the restaurant and had drank a little bit too much alcohol. I couldn't blame him though; Khreeo had flirted with Ricky shamelessly all evening. The last straw had been when Khreeo decided to announce that she feels she needs a break from their relationship. In response Kephern had said she should take a flying leap. At this point Ricky had decided to stand up for Khreeo and of course that had only added fuel to the fire.

"Why don't you leave the lady alone?" Ricky had interjected

"It seems to me that you have had a little too much to drink, I'm sure that you're not usually that rude to her."

"Why don't *I* leave the lady alone? I'll tell you why. *It's none of the your damn business!*" Kephern had sworn.

"If you weren't such an old man I'd have knocked you into next week. That should teach you not to stick your nose where it doesn't belong."

Of course it was obvious that the situation was getting out of control and both Dad and Linc had tried to put a stop to it. Unfortunately both Ricky and Kephern didn't pay any attention to what either one of them had to say. The situation further escalated when Kephern jumped to his feet at the table, knocking over some drinks, and poked his finger into Ricky's chest. Oh no! I thought to myself, it's definitely on now. At this point Dad called the waiter over and asked for our bill. He paid it and we all tried to make a hurried exit before we got thrown out. Surprisingly enough I didn't feel embarrassed or annoyed that my close friends were ruining my birthday dinner. Everyone blames Khreeo for being the catalyst that produced the spark. Needless to say though, she tried to be flippant about it, until Lynn and Ryoko gave her a talking to. Because Khreeo stubbornly remained rather contrite about the incident, I suspect she'd planned this all along. It suddenly brought back memories of a couple of incidents from college.

Khreeo had shown that she could be rather catty and calculating in her romantic endeavors.

"I'm surprised Khreeo" Ryoko had said,

"If you had told me that you needed something to spend your energy on I would have taught you the arts of origami or ikebana!"

"Maybe you could even buy her a bonsai tree," Kephern offered.

"She'll probably treat that inanimate object better than a real person"

"Enough Kephern, let's get out of here we're causing a scene. Not to mention that you and Khreeo and Ricky have ruined my wife's birthday." Linc admonished angrily.

I whisper into Linc's ear as we walk out of the restaurant. I let him know that I am fine but I didn't want him to get angry. I spend the entire drive home trying not to go over the unpleasant events of the evening. I chose rather to dwell on the niceties. Like when Carla had teased Linc and I about our trip to London and other parts of Britain for our honeymoon. She had even mimicked the English hotel operator she had spoken to on the one occasion she had called from America.

"Good afternoon madam, the gentleman and his wife have taken a stroll along the river Thames." The man had told her.

"Really?" Carla had teased.

"Are you sure Mr. Caldwell is a gentleman? Are you sure he's not a -------how do you say-------bloke, chap, lad, fella or even a rotten scoundrel?" she had continued, laughing in the poor man's ears.

"Not at all madam." He had replied,

"Mr. Caldwell has been a perfect gentleman. Remarkable manners I might add."

We all laughed at Carla's rendition of the English accent. She had even come up with a limerick she'd just heard.

"Let me tell you this new limerick I heard from an Irish friend a few days ago" she had announced loudly, in between drinks and desert.

"Is it clean enough for the dinner table?" Dad queried.

"I'll clean it up a little."

Before we could say 'Jack Robinson' she had plunged ahead.

"There was a young man from Bath
Whose --------were made of brass
He fell down a ladder
And clanked them together
So sparks flew out of his arse!"

I could only stare at her in stunned disbelief. I'm not a prude or anything like that but I was certainly thrown at *that*! Carla's little poem or limerick or whatever you want to call it, had certainly added an opposite effect to the prayers we'd said before we had begun our meal. I could only hope the people at the next table hadn't overheard her. Otherwise they would probably wonder how this seemingly

Christian-like group could pray before their meal, sing a hearty 'Happy birthday', only to tell dirty little jokes at the tail end of their gathering. Not to mention the swearing and fighting! A couple of people laughed but I think most of us were embarrassed because Dad was present. He seemed to take it in his usual stride though because he just smiled and said,

"You young people of nowadays can't seem to hold your wine very well. Good thing your mother isn't here Sydney or she'll probably have fainted in indignation."

We all knew that Mama is not that fragile by a long shot, but the way Dad said it made everyone laugh. Linc and I encouraged Khreeo to spend the night with us. She'd broken up with Kephern so she really didn't have a choice anyway. After that was settled, Carla drove us to Dad's hotel. We said goodnight to him and made a couple of arrangements for tomorrow, then Carla took Linc, Khreeo and I home.

It is close to midnight by the time Linc and I finally settle into bed. I cuddle up to him while he rests his hand on my belly.

"Now that's what I call a long evening sweetheart. Wouldn't you?" he whispers.

"Talk about drama abounding."

I laugh and squeeze him closer.

"Well it's certainly a birthday I'll always remember. Could we have foreseen any of this? I really don't know what to think about Khreeo jumping ship in a way that she knew would embarrass Kephern."

I know Ricky's not complaining now but I *know* him very well. He's not going to forget how Khreeo acted tonight and believe me he's no pushover. I bet he's thinking right now, that if she could do that to Kephern, she could possibly do the same to him one day."

"Hmm. I think you're right Linc." I respond.

"She may be remorseful in a day or two but let's talk about something else. On the way home from the restaurant I was wondering if we could go back to London for a couple of days next month. Maybe around Christmas or the new year."

Linc looks at me and smiles.

"I see a twinkle in your eyes young lady" he says.

"Seems to me that you fell in love with that little old island. Is it the fish and chips or the red double-decker buses? Or maybe it was 'Beauty and the Beast' the play we saw in Leicester Square."

"Actually it's all of the above," I laugh.

"I think Adam will be back from his vacation a week before Christmas and CSD will be closed from the 24th to the 26th and from the 31st to the 2nd of January. Which means I can get away from the around the 23rd of December till the 2nd."

Linc gives a deep sigh before replying. Meanwhile I had begun to go through his itinerary in my mind before he actually said a word.

"Well we break up for the Christmas vacation on the 18th so maybe we will go to London after all. We'll need to check with Dr. McKenna to make sure it's safe for you to air travel."

"Sounds like a plan honey. I'll call Dr. McKenna tomorrow and inform him." I conclude.

"Okay Sydney, right now though I just want to sleep. I've got a full day tomorrow at college. I've also got to finish your Dad's painting by Sunday so he can take it back to Boston with him. So snuggle up a little closer and I'll try to sleep off. Goodnight sweetheart."

Linc kissed me and within minutes he's fast asleep. I on the other hand am very excited. I truly did love England. I had loved Spain also; it seems that Europe is the place to vacation, at least in my opinion. Linc and I had stayed for a week at 'The London Metropole', which was just a stone's throw or bus ride if you like from the West End. The West End consists of Leicester Square, Piccadilly Circus, Marble Arch, Oxford Circus, Trafalgar Square and a host of other tourist attractions. Buckingham palace, Big Ben and the famous London Bridge are other great London attractions. We went to 'Madame Tussauds', the famous wax museum on Marylebone road. There are literally hundreds of wax figures of entertainers, politicians, royalty from around the world, athletes, actors, actresses and the list goes on and on. I recall how life-like they are. The workmanship on these wax figures is amazing.

Of course when you go to England you have to eat fish and chips, which can be bought just about anywhere. Cod was our favorite. We got to eat it the traditional way, walking along while eating the fish and chips out of newspaper cuttings. I was also fascinated with the red double-decker buses and the funny shaped black cabs. Of course the fact that they drive on the wrong side of the road and eat boiled tomatoes as part of their full breakfast, only confirms that the English really are *batty!* Two regrets that I hope to remedy on my next trip to England are to meet a *real* old English butler and go to the Royal Albert Hall. All over London you feel the sense of ancient history. True, in some parts of the city there is a merging of the past and the present but England's 900+ years of history was apparent to me nearly everywhere. Some days we'd catch the #16 bus from the hotel to Marble Arch and Oxford Circus. A couple of times we had walked along Edgware road (which is where the London Metropole is located). We'd stop to look at all the various shops and restaurants along the road. We ate at various English, Mediterranean and African restaurants and enjoyed all of them. At one Mediterranean restaurant we had char grilled rump of lamb with roast vegetable couscous and hot ginger treacle pudding with toffee sauce and ice cream for desert. *Now that was a meal and a half!* Another memorably scrumptious meal we'd eaten was roast pepper timbale (pastry) filled with mousse of goat's cheese, followed by cod served with orange and chili flavored sauce with pudding. What neither Linc nor I could bring ourselves to try though was Haggis, a Scottish meal comprising of offal and vegetables cooked in a sheep's stomach. Other than that we were fine. Linc also said he feels the pastries and deserts are nicer in Europe. The one week we had spent in London before going on to Sussex had not been long enough. There are a ton of things we didn't see and places we couldn't go to. The zoo, Big Ben, and the House of Parliament to name a few. Tottenham Court Road with all its electronic stores was another of Linc's favorite visits. There are dozens of stores selling all kinds of state of the art electronic gadgetry ranging from home and car stereos and alarms to cameras and computer equipment.

I'm certainly looking forward to a return visit to England, maybe this time I will get to ride the underground trains more often. I just hope Dr. McKenna does not forbid me to travel in my condition.

Sussex, where we had spent just three nights in Hartfield, had been heavenly. We had taken the train from Liverpool Street Station or was it Paddington? Oh! I can't remember. What I do remember is that we arrived early in the morning. Hartfield is a little village and we stayed at a tiny hotel called 'Bolebroke Mill'. A.A. Milne the creator of 'Winnie the Pooh' had once lived in Hartfield. Our room had been Elizabethan, with a big heavy wooden door and a four-poster bed. As far as the food…… I can't believe I'm thinking about food this much, because here I am remembering one of the breakfasts we'd had at the hotel. Mushrooms stuffed with bacon with melted cheese and pancakes stuffed with fruits. I think my appetite has been boosted. It must be these babies I'm carrying!

I think I need to get some sleep too. It's very late and although tomorrow is Saturday, I'll probably wake up when Linc does. Or maybe Khreeo will wake me up. I check that the alarm is set for 7.30am and close my eyes.

CHAPTER 19
LINCOLN CALDWELL

Monday, December 1st
Bronx, NY

If this were a book the reader would most likely want to know my take on the events of Sydney's birthday two weeks ago. Dramatic and surprising would be two words I would use to describe *that* evening. Ricky and Khreeo have seen a lot of each other over the past two weeks, how long it'll last is uncertain. Meanwhile, Kephern had immediately returned to Boston, a once angry man, but now feeling relieved. At least that's what he said. In all honesty I do feel that his break up with Khreeo is for the better. My sister Lynn has gone back home to Atlanta and the rest of the gang has settled down into their normal routines. Sydney had spent most of the following day with her father at his hotel. I had been busy on campus and hadn't returned home till after 5pm. I'd then spent a couple of hours on Mr. Collins painting. Sydney hadn't wanted to spend the day at home by herself and so had gone to meet up with her father at the hotel. The next day I had driven Mr. Collins to the airport, and then rushed back home to pick Sydney up and head to church. For Sydney and I the past couple of weeks have been fun. I've even been able to get her on the Harley Davidson for a five-minute ride. I taught Sydney how to ride a motorcycle last year and she's enjoying riding and has got over her initial apprehension, hence the boldness for a five-minute pregnancy ride.

As I contemplate over my life, I realize that in the past it had been my paintings and music respectively, which had been my loves. I'd been content to a point but I had been yearning for a family of my own to really be complete emotionally. I look forward to the pitter-patter of tiny feet. As professor of creative writing at Fordham, I have been able to help mold and motivate quite a few young men and women who have come across my path. I love teaching and have always interacted well with both my peers and my students. Sydney has accompanied me to a few functions over the past few years and has met a number of my colleagues as well as a few students and everyone seems to think highly of this young woman I married. Personally, I am very proud of my beautiful, intelligent, strong and *often very direct wife*. Depending on the occasion, I sometimes smile or may have to grimace when I recall certain incidents or conversations with Sydney. Sadly, the only downside to our marriage is that Valerie, Sydney's mother, is still openly hostile towards me. Valerie's treatment of Sydney isn't much better either. In fact she didn't even call to say happy birthday to Sydney last month. The first time we'd heard from her in a while was just a few days ago. At least that had been a phone call to find out about Sydney's health and the babies'. Thinking of babies, Sydney and I have already completed the babies' room. We've used light blue, yellow and red as the color scheme for the wallpaper, beddings and furniture. Sydney has convinced me that these colors would be fine whether the babies were boys or girls. I think I'd like to know what sex they are now, but I've agreed to wait till they are born. To say I am thrilled about becoming a father is an understatement. Aside from my wedding day, the day the twins are born will be the happiest day of my life.

I glance at the clock on the wall in my office just as my secretary's voice came through on my intercom.
"Professor Caldwell, there's a call for you on line 2. I tried to take a message, but the person insists on speaking with you. He says it's urgent."
"That's fine Irene; I'll take the call, thanks."
At this very second my cell phone starts ringing to. What's going on, I think. I quickly buzz my secretary back.
"Irene, please keep that call on hold. I have to answer my cell phone first, it may be my wife."
I grab my cell phone from out of my jacket pocket. For some reason my heart has started pounding fast and I am suddenly overcome with a feeling of gloom.
"Hello, Sydney is that you?" I ask.

"Mr. Caldwell, is that Mr. Caldwell?" the voice queries.

"Yes this is Caldwell speaking, who is this?"

"Mr. Caldwell, I'm glad I was able to reach you. This is Jim from EMS, (Emergency Medical Services)......... I have some news; it concerns your wife …"

CHAPTER 20
SYDNEY COLLINS-CALDWELL

Monday, December 1st
Manhattan, NY

I wake up in a sweat, I feel all wet and kind of sticky. What's wrong with me? I sit up in bed feeling a little panicky. I gasp as I feel a gush of blood that immediately soaks through my sheets and beddings. I'm immediately overcome with fear, and I scream!!! Oh! My God, how could this be happening? I just keep thinking--- I don't want to lose my babies, please God, help me! As I roll out of bed I notice that the mattress is also soaked through. I fumble for the phone and try to dial 911. I am struggling to remain calm but I'm so scared that for a few moments I don't realize that I have been dialing 999 instead of 911. I finally get through to the emergency operator and explain my situation. I am also concerned about how I'm even going to get up to open the door for the ambulance crew. Oh! My God, I need to call Linc; I'd better try the cell phone.

Why is it just ringing, where is he, why hasn't he picked it up? As I struggle to get out of bed, I keep on dialing. I realize that getting to the door isn't going to be easy, what's going to happen when the paramedics arrive? A few minutes later the doorbell rings repeatedly. I know it must be the ambulance crew, so I begin crawling to the door. As I drag myself along the floor, I could see a trail of blood behind me. I finally get to the door and gather my blood soaked nightie in one hand while I reach up from the floor to open the door. I'm too afraid to stand upright because I feel sure that the blood would gush out even more profusely. I'm weak and obviously very concerned about my babies. As I open the front door, one of the paramedics steps over me and into the apartment. The other man immediately kneels down to attend to me.

"Are you in any pain?" he asks

"No." I reply

I go on to tell him that my hospital bag is packed and in the bedroom. The man who had stepped over me hurries to the bedroom to grab it.

"Do you think you've lost the babies?"

I think for a moment before answering.

"I don't think so. I've obviously lost a lot of blood but I don't think that I've aborted the babies."

The other paramedic returns with my bag and the two of them help me onto a stretcher. As they wheel me toward the elevator I shout out for my cell phone.

"I think I've dropped my cell phone by the door. I haven't been able to reach my husband yet and I need to let him know what's happening."

One of the men retrieves the phone for me. He notices it is actually still dialing.

"The number you dialed last is still ringing Mrs. Caldwell."

I suddenly feel too dizzy to speak. I only *just* manage to tell him to ask for Mr. Caldwell and to let him know where they are taking me. It seems like from somewhere in the distance I could hear him ask,

"Mr. Caldwell, is that Mr. Caldwell?"

I had blacked out, God knows for how long. I have woken up in a hospital bed but I don't know which hospital I am in. I still feel very weak. As I turn my head to view my surroundings, I notice that I am attached to a machine monitoring the babies' heartbeats. In addition to the monitor I am also attached to a drip. A few moments later a doctor walks into my room with Linc following closely behind. I could tell from Linc's expression that I must be in better shape than I fear. He has a slightly worried look on his face but he still manages to smile as he approaches me.

"Hi sweetheart, how are you feeling? You scared us all for a minute there but the doctor says you should be fine with plenty of bed rest."

He bends over and gives me a big hug. I could see traces of tears in his eyes.

"Oh honey, I was so scared. I've never been so scared in my life. Are the babies okay?" I manage to splutter.

"Mrs. Caldwell, I'm Dr. Hill, I can tell you that your babies are fine. You lost a lot of blood and you'll be weak for a couple of days. Aside from that, there are a couple of things I would like to discuss with both you and your husband." The doctor interjected.

"I'll leave you alone with your husband for a few minutes but I'll be back shortly."

With a curt nod to Linc, Dr. Hill leaves the room.

"Don't get worried sweetheart, I'm sure the doctor just wants to give us some guidelines to possibly prevent this from reoccurring." Linc says, with a little grin.

I take a deep breath and adjust myself in the bed.

"I hope you're right Linc, I hope you're right."

"I'm sure I am; besides we have nothing to worry about remember? More importantly than the prescribed bed rest all we need to do is pray. I'm sure God hasn't brought us this far only to desert us now! Right?"

"You *are* right Linc. This is the first time I'll ever have anything physically wrong with me, I must have panicked."

"There *isn't* anything physically wrong with you sweetheart, you're pregnant that's all."

I nod in agreement and think about the fact that it is true. *I am pregnant!* I don't have an incurable disease that needs extensive rehab or some unspeakable illness. I also must not forget the importance of what Linc has just said. I have God to look up to! I remembered one of my favorite Psalms. Psalm 121, which reads 'I will lift up mine eyes unto the hills, from whence cometh my help? My help cometh from the Lord, which made heaven and earth.' I smile to myself because I always wonder why whenever I recall biblical scripture; it is in the King James Version! It must be because when I first became born-again it was a KJV bible that I had been presented with by the Pastor of my college. I begin to calm myself down; all I really do need to do *is* follow the doctor's instructions *and* pray. A few moments later Dr. Hill walks back into the room. He comes over to my bedside and looks down at me. I find myself smiling again.

"Glad to see you're feeling better, even in a smiling mood" he says.

I couldn't stop myself from laughing out loud. Both Linc and Dr. Hill are now looking at me with puzzled expressions on their faces. Linc manages to speak first.

"What's so funny sweetheart?" he asks.

"I'm sorry guys, I had just been recalling Psalm 121 from the bible and here I am, looking up to the hill (Dr. Hill)."

"Well I'm flattered Mrs. Caldwell. I hasten to add though that I'm far less of a physician than the Almighty." Dr. Hill replies grinning.

Linc bends down and gives me a kiss on my cheek.

"With your help Dr. Hill and that of the Almighty's, I'm certain we'll get through the next 3 months of this pregnancy."

"With flying colors I presume." I add with a wide smile.

"You presume correctly Mrs. Caldwell. Here at St. Patrick's Hospital we provide the best possible care, however if you have a preference for any other hospital, that does not present a problem at all. Under the circumstances you will need complete bed rest for the term of the pregnancy. But you may be moved to another location of your choice by tomorrow. Your husband has contacted your own doctor and I spoke with him too, he'll be calling soon. Let me explain the details of your condition."

I hold up my hand for a second.

"I hope this isn't bad news Doctor." I almost whisper.

Linc sits down next to me on the bed and gives me a little squeeze.

"It'll be okay sweetheart." He says.

I give a deep sigh and motion for Doctor Hill to continue. Before he could say anything though, I hurriedly add

"Err doctor, regarding whether or not I'll stay at this hospital I think we'll discuss it and let you know later on today. Would that be okay?"

"Certainly. There's no rush. Actually the longer you remain here the more rest you'll get. Subsequently the stronger you'll be should you decide to relocate." He replies.

Dr. Hill continued, "What I have to say is very important so listen up. The news isn't very good but it isn't all bad either. You have a low-lying placenta, otherwise known as placenta-previa. This just means that your placenta is covering all or part of the birth canal exit. I'm aware that you are familiar with the condition because your doctor (Dr. McKenna) mentioned to me that you had a tiny scare 3 weeks ago. He said you bled slightly and during an examination and ultra-sound scan he confirmed to you that you have placenta-previa. I understand you've been working off and on during the past 3 weeks, which of course is a big, no no! I'm sure Dr. McKenna advised you to quit work, right?"

I nod sheepishly. "Yes he did," I answer.

Dr. Hill continues.

"For the next 12 or so weeks of your pregnancy you are going to need to stay in bed 24/7. A good portion of the time you'll also have a monitor attached to you as well as a drip."

I look around the room, my mind drifting off into silent despair. 24 hours a day in a strange bed, in a hospital ward? This is not turning out to be the picture perfect pregnancy I had been fantasizing about. What happened to my looking all beautiful and cool and elegant up till the delivery day? I had imagined calmly putting on a little make-up when my labor starts and then heading out the door for the hospital. Now it seems I'm doomed to this room or one just like it for the next 3 months and worse still, I'll also have wires and needles sticking in and out of me.

"Oh God, I'm not doing this again." I mutter under my breath.

I catch Dr. Hill grinning at me.

"I really don't see the humor right now doctor." I mutter again.

"It isn't that bad Mrs. Caldwell, both babies are fine and I'm sure that you'll settle in very well. You'll be surprised just how well things will turn out eventually. By the way Mr. And Mrs. Caldwell, do you know the gender of your babies?"

"No we don't and we'd like to keep it that way till they are born." Linc answers.

"Great, I'm going to leave the two of you for a while. I'll pop round again in a few hours. The nurses will be constantly checking up on you and the babies. Okay?"

I just stare at him without answering. It is Linc that bids him farewell. I could only brood over my situation and try to think of something that might cheer me up. I also remember what Dad always tells me------that maturity has more to do with the types of experiences you've had and what you've learned from them and less to do with how many birthdays you've celebrated! So what am I learning from this experience? One thing I've learned for sure is that you are not always in control of what is happening to you.

I take a deep breath and sigh; I suppose the best thing for me to do now is try to settle down. However I think I will change hospitals. At least I'll be in more familiar surroundings. Maybe Dr. Hill is right -----that as long as my babies are healthy I'll do just fine.

Linc bends over me and kisses me on my cheek. I could see his forehead furrow, as it usually is when he's deep in thought. His handsome features set in a concerned look. I know instinctively that he is more worried about my emotional state than my physical state. During the past 2 years of marriage I have found my husband to be quite confident of the abilities of medical doctors. It is psychiatrists and psychologists that he is unsure of. Linc feels, and understandably so, that healing the physical body is a totally different ball game from delving into the psyche and minds of people. I on the other hand have my confidence in the healing power of God's promises in the bible. A poem suddenly forms in my mind............

> In God we trust
> Fear not I say
> With faith we must
> At all times pray.

All of a sudden I feel elated, my spirit lifts. Now I know what I would spend most of my time doing. I'll compile my poems into a journal and see how many new ones I could add on a weekly basis. I'll also be able to study my bible daily, I won't have the excuse of being too busy. I know instinctively that reading my bible will rid me of any fears I may have regarding my condition. The bible tells me that Jesus died for my sins and also for all of my *infirmities*, that He is my

Jehovah Rafah (the Lord my healer), that He is the healing balm of Gilead and that the shedding of His blood has washed me free of sin and death! What then do I have to fear? ***Absolutely nothing!***

"You know what Linc? I think I'll do just fine after all. I'll do a lot of reading and writing. You're going to have to bring me a lot of meals because I'm sure I won't survive on hospital food."

Linc bursts out laughing.

"Food? You're thinking about food? Here I am worried about you and you are already planning your menus."

"I love you too sweetheart" I respond

"I think if I'd hire a tall, dark, handsome firefighter as my personal secretary like I'd wanted to, he won't mind bringing me meals from Dante's."

"Probably, but the meals could end up either soaked with water or burnt, before they got to you." Linc replies, a mischievous grin on his face.

"Uh huh."

"I think we should call up the gang and let them know what's going on, don't you agree?"

"You're right sweetheart, maybe I'll even get a couple of visitors today. Are Woody and Lola back from their vacation in New Orleans yet?" I ask.

"And isn't Carla in New Jersey somewhere?" I add.

"Slow down honey, Carla *is* back. I'm not sure about Woody and Lola though. Do you want to call them yourself?"

"Yep, it'll take my mind off things. I'll also call Dad okay? Linc, sweetheart, do you think you'll be able to bring me a Cadbury's milk tray later?" I query.

"Alright baby, but you'll have to promise me that you won't overdo the sugary stuff. However, if you do put on 500 pounds I'll still love you…..*maybe!*" Linc laughs.

"Yeh right!!"

CHAPTER 21
SYDNEY COLLINS-CALDWELL

Thursday December 11th
Manhattan, NY

Ten long days, that's how long I've been stuck here. Some days have been good others have been downright horrible. I have had pain, bleeding and apprehension keeping me company hours at a time. My intention had been to move hospitals but I had changed my mind within the first couple of days. I've become comfortable with this hospital and its staff and Dr. Hill has been very good. Dr. McKenna has called me several times and although I may still move from here, at least I'm fine for now. The gang has been over to see me often, which has helped a lot. My major discomfort with being here in hospital is boredom. I've written a couple of poems and read dozens of magazines and two or three books but I've still found some time left over to be bored. However there has been a bit of drama over the past few days due to a surprise visitor.....namely Omar.

I hadn't heard or seen Omar in quite a while, so his showing up here was a big surprise. Not necessarily a welcome one but I was at least a little glad to see a couple more familiar faces. He had shown up with Kephern and after the initial pleasantries and show of concern over my well being they had both put their battle faces on. Carla had been with me at the time and that was a good thing too. The drama started as soon as Omar started being sarcastic about Linc and to make matters worse Kephern had chipped in, in agreement.

"So *where* is this *wonderful* husband of yours?" Omar had asked

"Yeah, it's 8 p.m. and you said he hasn't been here to see you today. What's up with that?" Kephern had added.

I immediately began to seethe inside. Who do they think they are? Coming in here to see me on my hospital bed and then have the nerve to berate my husband. Whether Linc has been here all day every day is none of their business! Luckily Carla had a response before I could open my mouth.

"You two had better leave if you're going to upset Sydney. Come on guys your 15 minutes of grace is up."

"Hey, I wasn't asking after *your* husband Carla--------or what is her name anyway?" Omar asks, turning to Kephern.

"Oh no you didn't, my God! You really are a piece of work Omar. I'm going to get the nurse to throw you out right now" Carla responded angrily.

I had put my hand on her arm and said

"It's okay Carla; I've already pressed the bedside alarm the nurse should be here any second."

"Really? You surprise me Syd. First you marry some old guy that you had only just met and secondly, in addition to running off to Europe with him on vacation, you go against your mother's wishes in everything relating to this guy. Now you're holed up in hospital with pregnancy complications and he can't even bother to see you everyday. This wouldn't have happened if you'd married me. What happened to all those plans for the future that you and I had dreamed about?"

"What part of I didn't love you don't you understand or remember Omar? I don't recall you and me *ever* discussing marriage. Are you crazy? Didn't my marrying someone else tell you something? I had told you a hundred times before I got married that you are just a good friend. I had even told you *that* long before Linc ever came into the picture. I thought that even your thick skin would eventually take no for an answer."

"Good friend? Just a good friend? Is that what you call me now? It wasn't what you called me during several particular nights we spent together. Does *wonderful* husband Linc know that? I'll tell you something else too. You may be married to someone else right now but you're still going to be *my* wife someday."

By this time I was ready to scream at him. I was literally shaking in my bed.

"Get out, get out Omar and drag your sorry friend with you. I cannot believe that I once thought you would grow up into a man. You're nothing more than an immature boy and if I could get out of this bed quickly enough I'd smack you upside your sorry head. And for the record *you and I never shared any passionate nights or days together*, not to mention me ever referring to you in any special romantic way. Boy am I glad about that! As for you Kephern-------obviously Khreeo is better off with Ricky."

I had been shouting at them and the nurses had heard. Three of them were now in my room trying to calm me down while hustling Omar and Kephern out.

"You can't over excite yourself Mrs. Caldwell." One of them was saying repeatedly.

"Calm down, remember just yesterday you were bleeding again." Another nurse had added.

"I came to New York just to see you. I'm going to be around for a while so you'll be seeing me again." Omar said as he was finally shoved out of hearing.

"Unbelievable." Carla remarked.

"If I hadn't been here I wouldn't have believed it. Linc is going to be mad when he hears about this."

One of the nurses interjected in a concerned tone.

"I think you shouldn't dwell on this too much Mrs. Caldwell. Your babies' heart rates have increased, as you can see from the monitor."

"I'll be fine nurse, thanks."

"I hope so." Carla adds.

"You still look pretty angry. Not that I blame you but I don't think Dr. Hill would have prescribed this kind of excitement. I know he wouldn't want you going through any emotional anguish at this time. Omar's behavior stems from the fact that he's still smitten with you Sydney, even after two years. Being married to Linc hasn't stopped him from still caring for you either. Now what did he mean by you're still going to be his wife?"

"I have no idea and I don't really care. As far as I'm concerned he can threaten to throw himself off the Empire State building and I still wouldn't marry him. In other words I wouldn't even marry him to save his life!"

Carla started laughing. As usual she had found some humor in what was said or done around her. It was amazing to me that Carla was still single. She has the biggest heart of gold I'd ever seen in one person.

"Why are you not married Carla? I know I've asked you this before but I just can't get over why any man would pass you up."

"Oh come now Sydney, it's obvious why. Look at me I weigh about a ton. It seems not many *brothers* want a woman they can't pick up. *And most* men I meet are scared of me. Think about it, they see me on stage and even though I don't usually pick on audience members, people generally, even the women, are quite apprehensive around me."

"I don't buy *that* at all, lots of *brothers* like big women, especially African *sisters* with a butt like yours."

Of course we both burst out laughing and for a minute or two I had forgotten about Omar.

"Well you just show me where *these* brothers are and I'll head down there like a shot out of a .44 magnum."

"Sounds pretty eager to me Carla, where is your dignity girlfriend?" I continue jokingly.

" Digni…what? Forget that. Like I said just show me the beef."

We both crack up. We are still laughing when Dr. Hill walks in.

"Good. You seem to be in brighter spirits Mrs. Caldwell. Hello Miss. Carla, how are you today? Have you been taking care of my patient or have you been instrumental in getting her upset?" Dr. Hill asks smiling.

"I'll be instrumental in putting an instrument in you, Dr. Hill, if you're not careful. Sydney, pass me that needle in your wrist and I'll see if our smiling doctor here can take what he gives out." Carla rejoined with an evil looking smirk in her eyes.

"I'd best stay clear of you then." He replies, taking good measure to walk around to the opposite side of my bed, way out of Carla's reach.

"Are you two playing with each other at my expense?" I ask.

"Shame on you Sydney, Dr. Hill is a happily married man." Carla replies, while trying to look genuinely shocked.

"How do you know that?" I ask, surprised.

As far as I know Dr. Hill isn't married. At least he doesn't wear a wedding ring. Now it is both of them that start laughing.

"It's okay Mrs. Caldwell. I had told Carla last week that I'm married. Remember the day she and I had met in the elevator? Well she had proceeded to query me about my life history and you know Carla better than I do. She didn't take no for an answer till she'd found out everything she wanted to. She even knows my shoe size!"

"*Carla!!*" I admonish. "I can't believe you did that."

"Psst, no biggie. I was just being the strong black woman. Besides he doesn't wear a ring how was I to know he isn't available?"

Carla really is something else. She sits on the chair looking as innocent as possible while managing to retain a gleam in her eyes. I couldn't help smiling and winking at her.

"Uh huh. I saw that. I'm going to have to report you to Lincoln." The doctor says, catching my wink.

"Now back to business young lady. How are you feeling? It seems the excitement hasn't really done you any harm."

I tell Dr. Hill that I feel fine. He stays on for a few more minutes before continuing on his rounds. Carla also stayed with me a while. She leaves around 10p.m after promising to call me the following morning. I am now left with my thoughts. Why hasn't Linc stopped by today? It is unusual and he hasn't called since noon. I pick up my phone and call home.

The phone rings and rings, no response. I try his cell phone and he still doesn't answer. I leave a message for him and settle down to sleep for the night. I am awakened 45 minutes later by a barrage of kisses on my cheeks and forehead. It is Linc.

"Hi baby. I'm so sorry sweetheart. Today has been the worst possible day at work."

"Hi honey" I answer groggily,

"What happened to you?"

"I've been in a couple of faculty meetings since I last spoke to you this afternoon. Then I had to go with Professor Mugweni to…… never mind, I'll tell you about the Professor's mishap some other time. I don't want you to get upset. I couldn't even call you. I can't find my cell phone. As far as I can recall it may be on campus or maybe I left it in one of the cabs I've been in today. I'm really sorry Princess. How have you been?"

"You won't believe what happened Linc".

From the expression on my face Linc decides he'd better sit down. He pulls the only seat over to the side of my bed and raises his eyebrows in anticipation. I take a deep breath and launch into the events of a short while earlier. As soon as I begin to recall Omar's rudeness, the anger comes back, sweeping all over my body. My eyes are alternating between Linc's face and the window. Also sometimes darting along the walls, basically I am fuming again. I don't even realize that during my revelation of events to Linc that I have lambasted Omar with some uncharacteristically unpleasant words. After what seems like ten minutes although it was only maybe three, I finish. I re-adjust myself in bed and stare at Linc.

"Wow! Talk about arrogance and foolishness. What's Kephern's problem? Obviously he's still mad at Ricky but why is he blaming us? He and Omar had better not come back. If I meet Omar here, there will be hell to pay. I thought the guy was over you by now; the man needs to grow up. Don't worry about him any more Sydney. We can inform the staff not to let them see you should they show up".

"You're right. Maybe we should do that. It'll save you the trouble of throwing him out on his ass. Although I wouldn't mind seeing you do that".

Linc smiles ruefully. I have a sneaky feeling he wouldn't mind getting physical, possibly even enjoy it. Other than regularly playing tennis and working out at our local gym three times a week, I haven't known Linc to be a violent person. However, I have seen him angry before and I get the impression that he'll feel confident throwing his 74inch, 215lb athletic frame around. Now it is my turn to smile to myself. I wonder what the outcome of such a conflict would be. Omar is a much younger man. He's a little shorter at 6ft and probably no more that 180lbs but if he's kept up his avid racquetball playing then he'll be very fit too. Hmmm, I think I'd put my money on Linc, Omar hasn't really ever shown confidence in any warrior type activity. Having two men fight over me had always seemed exciting, ever since

I was a little girl. But I certainly didn't want my husband to have to do that, especially if it involves aggravation from that jackass.

"Let's forget about those two for now sweetheart. I just want to get into bed with you but the bed is too small" Linc says.

"Hey, behave yourself sir. Look around you this room is pretty bare. There's nothing romantic other than all these flowers you've sent me over the past ten days and I don't think the nurses will appreciate what you have in mind either. *We* might be the ones to get thrown out on our asses!"

"Ha-ha I only want to hold your hand, you're the one with the naughty thoughts girl".

Linc does end up getting into bed with me that night and that's exactly where the nurse on duty finds him an hour later. Fortunately it is been one of the nurses familiar with us so she isn't complaining. She smiles at the sight of this big guy and his very pregnant wife on a single hospital bed. We obviously look uncomfortable and sheepish. She laughs and makes a few comments while examining me.

"It's a little after midnight Mrs. Caldwell, is your husband spending the night with you?" she asks.

"I'll be leaving in a couple of minutes Ma'am" Linc replies.

"I'll be back tomorrow Sydney. I'm not working so I'll be here practically all day. Okay? I should be here by 10 am".

I nod.

"Alright Linc. I'm really tired now anyway so I'll look forward to seeing you tomorrow."

After hugging me he rolls off the bed and kisses my belly saying goodnight to his babies. A few moments later both Linc and the nurse leave the room and I could hear him saying goodnight to a couple of other hospital staff as he walks down the hallway.

CHAPTER 22
SYDNEY COLLINS-CALDWELL

Monday December 15th
Manhattan, NY

"Hello everyone" a loud voice booms.

It is Dad. He's just arrived from Boston less than a couple of hours ago. Seeing him walk in brings a huge smile to my face.

"Dad!" I exclaim, obviously excited.

Most of the gang is also in my room with me. It is late evening and they have all stopped in from work. The only people missing are Linc and Ryoko. Dad comes over and gingerly hugs me.

"Hey baby girl you're looking good," he says.

"Yeh, yeh Dad, you're just saying that to make me feel good".

"No really! You look great. I mean you are what…seven months pregnant?"

"Yep, there about. I'm 29 weeks pregnant now. It seems like I've been pregnant forever though. Where is Mama?" I query.

"She's back home in Boston; she's got a group of associates coming over for some meetings. Sorry honey, that's why she couldn't make it this trip".

"Don't make excuses for her Dad. I know the real reason she's not here".

"Oh come on Sydney, chill out a little. I'm sure your mum will call later on," Lola admonishes.

Yeah that's right" Woody adds.

Anyway we all settle down to talk about everything under the sun. The nurses have brought in a few extra seats to accommodate the crowd and so most people are seated but Khreeo is sitting down on the edge of my bed. Woody and Lola have brought me some home cooking and I am eager to get started on the food. This is only the second time during the past two weeks that the gang has all met at the hospital, so we are all excited and having a good time. My side tables and shelves are always full of fresh flowers, cards, fruits and juices. In addition to what Woody and Lola have brought today, Khreeo and Ricky have come with chocolates and a bottle of wine. Why Ricky thinks I should drink a little alcohol escapes logic! In a few minutes Linc should arrive. I don't know where Ryoko is though.

"Where is Ryoko guys?" I ask.

"Don't know. Maybe she's working," says Carla.

Just at that moment there is a knock on my door. It is a nurse.

"Mrs. Caldwell your husband is here and so is a Mr. Thomas but your husband is refusing to let Mr. Thomas come through to see you. What do you want me to do? At the rate they are going someone might call security any second."

"Who's Mr. Thomas, Sydney?" Lola and Woody ask simultaneously.

"That's Omar. Ricky, I think you need to get out there real quick because Linc has threatened to throw Omar out if he shows up here again" I hurriedly reply.

"I'm on my way" Ricky responds as he jumps up and rushes out of the room with Woody in pursuit.

"What's going on? What's all that about?" Dad asks.

Khreeo, Carla, Lola and Dad all turn to look at me expectantly. Khreeo raises her eyebrows and Carla nudges me in my ribs with the expression on their faces saying, aren't you going to tell your father what happened?

"I'm sorry Dad. Omar had come over to see me a few days ago but he and Kephern had been very rude. Especially Omar, He had gone on about still wanting me even though I'm already married. He had also insinuated that Linc wasn't really as good a husband as I make him out to be. He had basically been more trouble than his visit was worth."

"I thought he had gotten over you. *I* haven't spoken to him for a couple of months but I know he and your mother speak to one another frequently."

"Well, he apparently hasn't gotten over Sydney and to make matters worse, it seems he's out to make trouble. I felt like smacking him myself." Carla injects.

"I'm actually concerned for Sydney's health. She really doesn't need all this emotional hassle right now."

"Ain't that the truth?" Lola concludes.

A few minutes later Woody, Kephern and Omar walk into my room. According to Woody, Ricky had convinced Linc to allow Omar and Kephern to see me for just a few minutes. Omar greets Dad politely but only nods to everyone else in the room. Kephern on the other hand has just glared at Khreeo as soon as he got inside. I am pretty confident that with a crowd of people present Omar would behave. And so I'm completely taken aback and unprepared when the next thing that comes out of his mouth is…

"Have you been thinking about what I said? I still love you and I don't care who knows."

Everyone in the room goes silent. Kephern is the next person to speak.

"Lucky you Syd, Khreeo on the other hand isn't so fortunate. I don't want you any longer Khreeo and I wouldn't touch you again not even with a ten foot pole."

"Well bring out the bells and break out the bubbly! And while we're at it lets also hire a cabaret!" Khreeo answers sarcastically.

"You can be as bitchy as you want Khreeo. Why you and Syd would throw yourselves at a couple of old guys is beyond me."

"Of course it's beyond you Kephern. Just like many other things in life are beyond you, our relationship being one of the obvious ones. Your inability to grasp emotionally demanding concepts is eventually going to cause your demise with any woman." is Khreeo's caustic addition.

"I really doubt *that*, girl. You're assuming all women are bitches like you, right?" Kephern scathingly retorts.

"Enough of this nonsense!" Dad exclaims.

"You people are bickering like children. Kephern you owe Khreeo an apology for calling her that…**B** word and….."

Before Dad could finish his sentence Khreeo was at Kephern's throat. She is tearing at his tee shirt and jacket collar while trying to scratch his neck and any other exposed flesh with her long sharp, nicely manicured fingernails. Talk about drama in the ER. We aren't exactly in the Emergency Room now but all this drama in my room could send me there pronto! While Woody, Lola and Carla are struggling to separate them, Omar in his infinite wisdom decides to come over and sit on my bed, close to me.

"What do you think you're doing Omar?" I practically yell at him.

"What? I can't sit next to you now?"

Dad comes over and asks Omar to leave. Khreeo has finally been dragged away from Kephern but she is still screaming obscenities at him. Omar it seems, hasn't had enough of an altercation because he proceeds to express loudly that he is going to show all of us how big of a mistake I had made marrying Linc. *His* error as it turns out is not getting up from the bed because Linc and Ricky walk through the door at that very moment! I think… 'Oh no.'

"Get the h… away from her Omar or I'll knock your ass out!" Linc shouts angrily.

"Or what…old man." is Omar's foolish reply.

Linc in his fury takes two long strides across the room and slams his fist into Omar's face. Blood splatters everywhere, on my bed sheets, Dad's suit, on my lamp and on Linc's clothing as well. Pandemonium breaks loose and all I can think about is Linc getting arrested and hope that Omar isn't seriously hurt. A bunch of nurses and a couple of doctors come bustling into the room, which suddenly feels very overcrowded. Omar is being attended to by two of the nurses and the two doctors are over at my side making sure I'm okay. Two security guards also run inside.

"What on earth is going on here?" asks Dr. Hill, standing at the doorway.

"Just a misunderstanding." Dad offers.

"Looks like a mighty big one Sir. Mrs. Caldwell, do you have an explanation for all this and where did all this blood come from?"

"It's from Mr. Thomas's nose Dr. Hill. It seems he was punched but it's not broken thank God." replies one of the nurses attending to Omar.

"Well that's the first bit of positive information I've been given so far."

The security officer who seems to be the higher ranking one asks...

"Is that what happened Mr. Thomas? Were you punched and *who* punched you?"

For a few moments everyone was dead silent. Just as it seems the officer was about to repeat the question Linc butts in.

"I did. I hit him."

Dr. Hill looks rather surprised at Linc's admission.

"Why?" the security officer asks.

"It's a long story; however the short version is simply that Omar...."

Omar himself, shocking the gang with what he says next, cuts Linc short.

"*You* didn't hit me old man. You may have thought about it but you'd be too slow to carry it out! Talk about if wishes were horses...."

With that, Omar stands up and straightens himself out. He and Kephern stride toward the door, turning around as they reach it.

"I hear you play chess too Linc so I'll put it to you this way. You've won rounds one and two with your opening gambit but my end game is very strong!"

Before anyone can say anything else he and Kephern are gone down the hall and out of sight. After a few more embarrassing moments of silence Khreeo has something to say.

"Phew, good riddance to bad rubbish. I thought they'd never leave what a couple of losers."

Everyone turns to look at her, including the two officers. Dr. Hill satisfies himself that I am alright and then leaves. The nurses arrange for the blood to be cleaned up and they leave too. The senior security officer is the last to leave. On his way out he stops in front of Linc and looks him in the eye.

"Lucky break man, I wouldn't count on being so lucky next time; I hope you regret what happened sir."

"Better believe it. It was out of character and I'm sure there are regrets all around." Linc replies.

After he leaves we all breathe a sigh of relief. I am not sure whether Omar hadn't pressed charges out of embarrassment or maybe he has other plans. I'm sure though that it wasn't out of the kindness of his heart. I look around me at my small but close-knit family and friends, even though it isn't a large group I still feel blessed. The only other important person in my life is Mama but I don't miss her. As mentioned before, my relationship with her needs work.

"I feel as if I've been in a time warp or something. Not déjà vu but.... Oh, I don't know....Linc, you remember how time was warped or should I say skipped back in 1752?" I ask.

"Sydney, now what are you rambling about?" Carla queries.

"I believe she's referring to September 1752. That's the weirdest month in modern day history. The calendar actually jumped from Wednesday 2nd September to the next day Thursday but it didn't become Thursday 3rd September it became Thursday 14th September. See! The calendar skipped 12 days!"

"Absolutely right Ricky." says Linc.

"Why did that happen?" asks Carla.

"Probably 'cos someone didn't like the 13th." Laughs Lola.

We all laugh.

"Good guess Lola but that's not the real reason. Apparently the calendar being used up to that date was called the Gregorian calendar but it had been proven to be inaccurate. The only possible way to correct it to the new Julian calendar was to skip those crucial days." Ricky continues.

"I wonder whether workers would have been paid for the whole month of September that year or would they have had their wages docked for those 12 disappearing days?" asks Carla jokingly.

"Back then I think people were forced to work 7 days a week. There were no union reps in those days." Dad volunteers.

The gang and Dad spent another 2 hours with me before preparing to leave. Two or three minutes ago Ricky had been called away to receive a phone call. He walks back into the room, his face looking ashen and downcast. What now I muse? I suddenly feel sick.

"Guys! That call was from one of Ryoko's colleagues. She's just been shot! And it's bad, she caught a blast from a double-barreled shotgun and even though she was wearing a Kevlar vest…"

CHAPTER 23
RYOKO YOKOZUNA

Monday December 15th
Manhattan, NY

How long am I going to do this for? I wonder. I've been shot, stabbed, sliced and diced at various times during my career so far. And to make matters a little worse, I have a bad feeling about this here gig.

It is broad daylight; I'm fully geared up with about fifteen of my SWAT team colleagues, poised to storm into this brownstone at the corner of 35th and Kenton Street. We've got the building completely surrounded and we know that there are five perps inside. I look up as I feel a rain drop on my face, damn, it looks like rain. I've never liked working in the rain, don't know why but just never have.

The perps have been silent over the last 3 minutes, not answering the phone or responding to the bull horn request to come out with their hands up. I can see Captain Grady getting agitated. His pockmarked face tightening up round the jaw line and his thick eyebrows deeply furrowed.

"What the hell are these bums up to?" Grady whispers in my ear.

"Don't know for sure Cap, maybe they're just waiting for our next move. They still haven't made any demands right? So *what are* we waiting for?" I respond

"Hey, you just stay put till I give the order, kapish?"

"Yes sir Captain sir…how about we…"

Right in the middle of my sarcastic response a couple of shots ring out. One of the shots ricochets off the fire hydrant to my right and smashes through the rear windshield of the parked red BMW in front of me. The perps follow on with a barrage of bullets that rip into the cars we are crouching behind. Some the bullets rip right through the vehicles, good thing we are behind the engine block.

"Hear that Ryoko? These muth……..s aren't playing, recognize that AK47?"

"Yep sure do."

"Alright guys we're going in. Move it!" Captain Grady booms.

We begin to cautiously move forward in standard formation, a hail of gunfire around us. The sky opens up and rain pours down causing our advance to slow a little. I reach the side door with two other guys and one of them pops a flash grenade through the window. I signal him to pop another one through for good measure, ready my M16 at my shoulder and count to three.

"Go, go, go….." I yell

We crash through the side door into the large kitchen. The three of us split, I take the left lane, along the kitchen wall. Moving rapidly but cautiously we make it to the Spanish style archway leading out of the kitchen. Peering around the archway frame, I see one of the perps crouched below one of the living room windows, firing out at the cops outside. He swings round as he hears us approaching and fires the AK47 in his hands. All three of us return fire at the same time, our rounds hitting him and slamming him up against the wall. He's dead before he hits the floor. I scope the rest of the room and give the signal to continue after ensuring that the room is empty. We can hear gunfire coming from other rooms in the house as we proceed.

Another perp fires at us from halfway up the stairs. He turns and tries to run up the stairs but trips. As he struggles to get up, the officer on my left shoots him right through the head. He spins round as he's hit and falls over the banister to the wooden floor below.

Two other SWAT cops come into the hallway five yards from our position.

"There's a dead bad guy back in the den." One of them says.

"We took out two of them here, means there's two unaccounted for." I reply.

"Heads up…" the same cop begins to say, as he slumps to the floor, shot in the neck.

We all dive for cover as more shots slam into the floor, furniture and wall around us. The fallen officer lay on the floor in the open, blood gushing out of his neck. The other two perps are firing rapidly at us, pinning us down where we are. I can't let him die like this. I tap the officer next to me on the shoulder and say...

"Come on we've got to pull him to safety, he's a sitting duck out there."

I then signal to the other two cops to give us covering fire.

As they shoot back, me and the other cop crouch down and rush over to the fallen officer. We reach him safely and I immediately put my hand over his neck wound. I look into his eyes and see that they are glazed over.

"He's gone into shock and lost too much blood, we've got to get him outside. Ok buddy you've got to carry him, let's go" I say to my partner.

He hauls the injured cop over his shoulder in a fireman's carry as I open fire at the perps holed up in what seems to be the dining room. We move rapidly back the way we had entered the house. Backtracking into the living room I hear the unmistakable sound of a shotgun blast. My colleague is partially lifted off his feet and both he and the cop he's carrying fall in a heap. At the same time I'm wheeling and rolling, firing in the direction of the blast.

Standing no more than ten feet away is another perp, someone had goofed up badly. There aren't five perps in the house there are six...or maybe even more.

I'm too late...maybe by just a fraction of a second.

The second blast from the perp lifts and slams me back into the wall. The pain in my left shoulder is excruciating, I feel as if a thousand hypodermic needles have been injected into my shoulder. My vest no protection at all.

Damn it, I've dropped my gun. Through a misty, dizzy haze of intense pain I desperately try to reach for my Glock. I see the perp walking over and I roll onto my side, wincing in pain.

This is it I tell myself, I'm not gonna reach my sidearm in time.

Less than a second later the perp reaches me and stands over me, pointing his shotgun right at my head.

"Screw you." I yell at him as I roll again.

The shotgun goes off with a loud boom and I feel myself floating off into Nirvana.

Everything goes black and from a distance I hear yells and more rapid gunfire as I pass out...

CHAPTER 24
LINCOLN CALDWELL

Tuesday December 16th
Queens, NY

They say when it rains it pours. There's a lot of truth in that old saying. I've spent the last 3 hours here at the hospital and I still haven't been allowed to see Ryoko yet. Sydney had let me leave with everyone else last night. We had all come to this hospital in Queens where Ryoko is. We had met a large group of her fellow cops here; apparently there are two other officers that had been shot during the same incident.

I still haven't been able to ascertain exactly what had happened, the cops are being tight-lipped about it. Woody had joined me here an hour ago and we are both nearly fit to climb the walls.

"What do you think is going on Linc?"

"Beats me man! If we were family we'd know by now, unfortunately neither one of us looks Japanese nor do we have the last name Yokozuna."

"Ryoko doesn't have any family close by does she?"

"No she doesn't Woody. The one relative of hers that I met a few years ago had been in New York on vacation from Osaka."

"How is Sydney? Did you get to speak to her a few minutes ago?"

"I did. Her father is there and she had just finished speaking to her mother. Sydney is being very strong. Actually she's been strong since the beginning of this pregnancy. Know what Woody? I'm beginning to feel as if I live in hospital too. I'm going to be running back and forth between two hospitals for the duration."

"Yeah, you're right but you don't have a choice. Good thing college is out for the Christmas holidays."

One of the cops starts walking over towards us.

"Hey, who are you guys?" he asks Woody and me, rather aggressively.

"We're Ryoko's friends" Woody responds

"Yeah? Ain't never laid eyes on you before…you cops?" he asks.

"No, just good friends" I respond.

"You'd better be, don't want no slick reporters hanging around for a story. You sure you ain't no reporters?"

"We're not reporters and we're not cops, we are just concerned friends. Okay man?" I remark, a little angrily.

I'm getting irritated with this cop's many questions; I just want to see Ryoko.

He stares at both me and Woody for a good 30 seconds then adds…

"Huh, yeah, you look alright to me so I'll let ya'll stay. But don't either of ya be a pain in the ass; me and my buddies over there ain't in the mood for dealing with assholes, kapish?"

"Hey man, could you tell us what really happened out there? We heard that two other cops got shot too" I ask.

"Yeah, sure did and we're gonna catch them sonsabitches that did it. They sure as hell ain't gonna get away with it." He says.

He then leans in to me and Woody and adds…

"Them gonna pay, yes them gonna pay real bad! Don't wanna be in their shoes when we catch up to them. Ain't no cop in the triborough area that won't first pump some lead into them, then ask questions much later."

"We feel you man, we feel you." Woody adds.

"Linc, look over there. Isn't that the doctor we saw speaking to the cops outside Ryoko's room earlier? Let's go and talk to him, maybe we'll get lucky and he'll tell us something useful." Woody remarks.

"Sure."

"Good talking to you man, hope the other two officers do well too." I say to the cop as me and Woody walk off.

We catch up with the doctor and proceed to bombard him with questions. He puts up both his hands to slow us down. All he could confirm is that Ryoko and two other cops had been shot at close range and all three of them are in intensive care. He also says that maybe we'll be able to see or speak with her in another couple of hours, although it is dependent on how quickly their initial recovery is going. Woody and I decide to go grab something to eat. We'll return soon and hopefully we'll be able to see Ryoko. I give Sydney another call from the lobby, give her an update and Woody and I walk out of the hospital into the New York cold.

CHAPTER 25
SYDNEY COLLINS-CALDWELL
Wednesday December 24th
Manhattan, NY
Christmas Eve

"My apologies once again Sydney, I've been in Texas for the past few weeks. Pastor Al has kept me abreast of your condition. I believe you last spoke with him on Monday?"

This is Pastor Vince speaking to me on the phone. He's the Assistant Pastor of the local church Linc and I have been attending quite regularly since we got married. The church is located not too far from our home. It isn't a huge church, there are about 3,000 members in all but that's the way I like it. A few members of the congregation that have been friendly with us over the past year have stopped by to see me in hospital. Most of them had brought varying regular gifts but one thing they had all done in common was pray for me before leaving, prayers ranging from 5 minutes to 20 minutes. A common feeling I've had after each prayer session was *peace*. Pastor Al, the senior pastor, is also a medical doctor and although he no longer practices medicine he's been very helpful with his advice. He's also been able to explain in layman terms what's been happening with my body. Anytime Dr. Hill and some of the other attending physicians had been a little too technical, I've been able to discuss it with Pastor Al and get more clarity and understanding. Pastor Vince however is the one that Linc and I see more often. At least before I became hospitalized and that's why he's apologizing right now.

"Yes I did Pastor. He had told me you wouldn't be back in New York till Friday, merry Christmas in advance."

"Merry Christmas to you too Sydney, how are you today? Still keeping your faith level high? Remember what the bible says....All you need is faith the size of a mustard seed and you can remove any mountain in your path and without faith you cannot please God."

"I remember *that* most times but not always, especially not when I'm in pain or if I'm bleeding. The doctors have told me that they are just trying to keep the babies inside for as long as possible. Obviously the longer they stay in the womb the greater their chances are when they come out. I feel as if I'm glued to the bed, I only get to walk around the ward for short sessions. *That* has been extremely difficult to handle. Can you imagine that Pastor?" I moan.

"Well you and Linc both turned down an invitation to play tennis the last time I asked. My impression was that you in particular didn't like any form of sports or exertion." Pastor Vince replies. I'm sure with a smile.

"Are you teasing poor me Pastor?"

"Don't say poor you Sydney. You are not poor; you are rich and blessed with all Heavenly blessings in Christ Jesus. Say Amen."

"Amen Pastor."

"So, when are these precious babies due?"

"We were originally given the 25th of February but by the way things are going there is no telling for sure. In all honesty it could have been last week."

"The important thing is that the babies are in the best of health when they are born, right?"

"By the way Pastor Vince do you remember Ryoko? You met her and Carla, our two friends that have come to church with us a couple of times." I ask.

"I remember them. Ryoko is the Japanese lady, the police officer, right?"

"Yes. Unfortunately I have some bad news. She was shot last week and she's been in hospital since then. It was pretty bad and she was operated on. The good news is that she's recovering well."

"It seems you all have been very busy during my absence. Have you been able to speak to Ryoko or not?"

"I haven't, I tried but at the time she wasn't taking calls. Linc has been seeing her regularly though, at least over the last week. Truth is Pastor he's been seeing her more often than he's been here to see me. I don't mean to sound uncaring but Linc and I have argued over this issue more than once. I've spoken to a couple of our close friends about it and they've tried to make me understand that Linc feels obligated because he and Ryoko used to date and are still very close friends. Plus she has no family in the country. Am I being oversensitive? I like Ryoko and we've gotten along well ever since I met her but I have on occasion felt a pang when I see how close she and Linc still are. She's even been here to see me six times before her incident. So you see why I feel horrible for being on Linc's case. Before I forget Pastor, there is also another issue with an old boyfriend of mine who's been causing trouble."

I feel like I have been rattling on for ages, Pastor Vince is silent for a moment.

"First of all Sydney, your feelings are your feelings and whether right or wrong you can't ignore them. So that means you have to deal with them, which you seem to be doing. After all if you don't know yourself, who do you know? When you say Lincoln has been spending more time with Ryoko than you, exactly what do you mean?"

I take a deep breath and continue.

"In the last week since Ryoko's been accepting visitors, Linc has been here every day except one day last week, however when he has been here it's only for an hour or less. I feel as if he leaves after an obligatory period when he's sure I'm okay physically. I've been surprised. He makes some excuse or the other and then he's out the door to see Ryoko. He usually spends 5 or 6 hours at a time with her."

"What did he say when you asked him about it?"

"That she's been through a serious life threatening situation and that he's the only one that she really leans on for strength. He even got a call from her on Monday while he was here with me, next thing I know he's gone."

"Tell you what, when I get back on Friday how about I meet Linc in your room and we can talk about this? You will also be able to tell me about this ex-boyfriend of yours too. For now I just want you to take things as easy as possible. Remember you've got two little ones to think about. Arrange it with Linc. I can be at the hospital by 4pm and so if it suits both of you I'll see you then. How does that sound?"

"Sound fine with me. I'll mention it to him when he comes in today."

"Good, let me pray for you before I hang up. Heavenly Father your daughter Sydney and her husband Linc need your grace. Your word says that your grace is sufficient for us. Father, the fruit of the womb is your blessing I ask in the name of Jesus that their blessing be multiplied abundantly. I declare that no weapon of the enemy fashioned against them shall prosper and every tongue that rises against them in judgment shall be condemned. Heavenly Father your word says that he who finds a wife has found a good thing and obtains favor from the Lord. We thank you Lord because Linc has found a good wife and obtained favor from you. Let this favor manifest in multitudes. I declare Heavenly Father that Sydney's body is healed; that her delivery will be graced with your presence and her attending physicians will be guided by the Holy Spirit. In Jesus name we pray. Amen."

"Amen. I say in agreement."

"Thank you Pastor. I'll look forward to seeing you on Friday. Maybe I'll hear from Pastor Al today too."

"Very likely Sydney, I'll be speaking to him in a few minutes myself. Good-bye and take care. May God's grace be with you."

I settle down to watch some television. I flick through the channels looking for CNN; I need to know what else was going on in the world. I finally find CNN and spend the next 30 minutes catching up with news. Slightly after 11a.m. I get a call from Woody. He's calling from across town, from the hospital where Ryoko is. After checking up on me he passes the phone to Linc who spends the next 10 minutes alternating between concern over *my* welfare and Ryoko's well being. After a while I get fed up.

"You know what Linc? If you're going to be at another woman's bedside while speaking to your bed-ridden wife, then you might as well not even bother." I say angrily.

"Sweetheart take it easy, I was about to tell you that I'm on my way."

"On your way? How is it that you went to see Ryoko first? Huh? Don't bother to come over here. Just stay where you are, you usually do anyway!" I continue.

"Don't be like that Sydney. You know I've explained why I spend this much time here."

"So you have and it has only served to show me how little importance you have placed in the well being of your wife and children compared to your ex-girlfriend. Amazing isn't it. For the first time in our marriage Linc, I'm disappointed, very disappointed and very angry too."

"I'm sorry Sydney. You know there is an old saying that goes 'it takes a minute to find a special person, an hour to appreciate them, a day to love them and an entire life to forget them.' I can't just ignore her sweetheart. One of the nurses on her ward told me yesterday that as soon as Ryoko opened her eyes after the operation, she specifically asked for me."

"That's all well and good Linc but I don't care about all that. I need you here. How many times do I have to tell you that? Other than the physical aspect of my condition there is also the psychological. Even Carla has spent more time here than you recently." I continue furiously.

"Okay Sydney, I'll get down there as soon as possible.'

"What does that mean? Are you coming right away?"

"I'll leave here in a few minutes."

I am so angry with Linc that I actually hang up the phone without saying another word. From the way our conversation went I can't say exactly when Linc is going to get here. Hopefully hanging up the phone on him wouldn't make matters worse. I wish I could get around easier. I rang for a nurse. My calling for a nurse is to find out if I would finally be allowed to get on the elevator and walk around on the ground floor of the hospital, maybe spend some time in the shops. The nurse arrives but she informs me that I'll have to ask Dr. Hill and he won't be in till later on this afternoon. The fact that it'll be Christmas day tomorrow isn't helping my mood either. As far I can remember this is the only time that I have ever spent Christmas Eve in hospital. I'll also be here for Christmas day and New Year.

Lola, Carla. Khreeo and Adam Whittaker show up, all at the same time.

"Hi Sydney, look at me, I've got the sole company of three beautiful women all to myself. Can't recall the last time *that* occurred, if ever." Adam announces cheerfully.

"Hello guys...."

I try to say more but I can't. I just break down and start crying. I cry and sob, everyone tries to console me but it doesn't help. I don't want to tell them what is wrong because Adam is here. Carla and Lola had discussed it with me before but I hadn't mentioned it to Khreeo. Lola has probably guessed and therefore signals to the others to give me some space. They all go out and stand just outside the door. Within a minute Lola comes back in and everyone else comes back 3 minutes later. Adam makes excuses about not being able to stay long. The women must have told him that they needed to talk woman talk.

"Sorry Sydney. I really have to run. I'll call you tonight. Love you." Adam says apologetically.

And with that he leaves.

"Okay girl, out with it. Talk to mama." Lola prods.

"Am I losing Linc to Ryoko?" I sob.

"Of course not girl, what nonsense is that? It's your hormones talking. I swear if I had a dollar for every time a girlfriend said or behaved in a funny way due to hormones, I'd be a millionaire a couple of times over." Laughs Lola.

I wipe away my tears and decide to spend as long as possible getting a reasonable explanation from the women around me now.

CHAPTER 26
SYDNEY COLLINS-CALDWELL
Wednesday December 24th
Manhattan, NY
Christmas Eve----continued

Two hours of conversation, which have included explanations, cajoling and pleads still hasn't consoled me. I am still angry and Linc still isn't here. I couldn't believe that even after my last conversation with him it has still taken him so long to not be here. I am now very angry with Ryoko too. I feel like finding out her room number then giving her an angry phone call. I can tell that Lola, Carla and Khreeo are also upset with Linc, especially Carla and Khreeo. Carla has even told me that she's going to go and see Ryoko this evening and she intends to speak to her about it. I have urged her not to, that I'd like to mention it personally but I think there's no holding Carla back.

One of my regular nurses has just left. She had checked me over and detached me from the baby monitor so that I can move around a bit. I decide to walk around the ward for some exercise. Within seconds I have all the women in tow.
"It's obvious that Ryoko still cares for Linc." Khreeo blurts out.
There is silence for a few moments.
"I believe you're right but I think it's plutonic." I respond
"*Plutonic?*" Carla asks laughing.
Everyone else begins laughing too.
"Well you guys know what I meant don't you? Anyway, whether platonic or plutonic he should be here with me, right?"
They all say, "Yes" together.
"I still think she really needs to not hold on too tightly to someone that's not hers. She had her chance." I grumble.
Khreeo starts laughing again, that is, until I glare at her.
"What's funny now?" I query.

"You should have seen the expression on your face; you looked like a spoiled little brat."

"I don't think I'm being spoiled................"

"Excuse me Mrs. Caldwell, you have a call." said a nurse that had caught up with us with a portable phone.

"I grab the phone from her, fully expecting it to be Linc on the line.

"Hey" I say into the receiver.

"Hello little girl" the big voice came back from the other end.

"Hi Dad....................."

I spend a few minutes talking to Dad and Mama. By the time I finish I'm ready to go back to bed. My entourage and I turn and begin to walk back to my room. Dad had promised to call me tomorrow, Xmas day, from Florida. He and Mama will be back in New York to see me by the New Year.

"Did your dad's call cheer you up any?" Carla queries.

"Yes Carla. Dad and Mama are in Florida, they'll be in New York next week."

"Good, because I have a joke for you. I figure it should cheer you up but since you're feeling better I'll save it for another day."

"Go ahead and tell us anyway Carla" Lola prompts.

"Okay then...what does it mean when a man is in your bed gasping for breath and calling your name?"

We all ponder over it for a few moments before giving up.

"We have no idea girl. What's the answer?"

"It means you didn't hold the pillow down long enough!" Carla bursts out laughing.

"Here's another one," she continues.

"What do you call a hand-cuffed man?"

"Hmm. You can call him...........wait a minute. What's he handcuffed to?" Lola prods.

"Could it be he's handcuffed to bed parts by any chance?" Lola continues, laughing too.

All of us are now laughing loudly.

"No, he's not cuffed to your bed posts woman; get your mind out the gutter. The answer to my riddle is...trustworthy! That's what you call a handcuffed man." Carla finishes.

We all continue laughing and fooling around for another few moments, till it is punctuated by a man's jocular voice coming from the door way.

"Ah ha, so that's why you're still single, girl. That type of attitude certainly won't endear you to any nice young man, at least not the ones here in New York."

It is Linc. He had come into the room while we were laughing and we hadn't heard him.

He is standing there in his black knitted top and green khaki pants. Looking quite nice and cool, I think to myself. He's also smiling. I ignore his gaze as he walks over to my bed and I instead turn to speak to Lola by my side. After perfunctory nods to the other girls Linc sits on my bed. He takes my hand and presses it to his face but I not having any part of it. I snatch my hand away and put it under the blanket. Carla, Khreeo and Lola are all silently looking on and I'm sure Linc is beginning to feel uncomfortable.

"Have you ladies been here long?" he asks.

No one answers him.

"Come on ladies. Am I in the dog house with all of you?"

Still complete silence.

"How about excusing Sydney and I, so we can discuss a couple of things?" he continues.

"No such luck buddy, you're going to have to do your groveling right here. And right now I would suggest!" Lola says sternly.

Linc smiles and turns back to me.

"Sweetheart...." he begins.

Linc spends the next twenty-five minutes apologizing to me and telling me how much he loves me. Of course I begin to melt after maybe just 6 or 7 minutes but I keep a hard face on. I want to see whether he would give excuses in favor of Ryoko. Fortunately he doesn't and so I'm willing to forgive but not forget, at least for the time being. We all spend the rest of the evening joking around and generally being as we usually are together as the 'gang', even Adam and Woody show up an hour later. Woody and Lola eventually leave first and Khreeo and Carla stay on but leave Linc and I alone for a while. We of course get round to talking about how Ryoko is coming along. Linc says she has improved and could possibly be out of hospital before the New Year came round.

"That sounds like good news for Ryoko." I comment.

"Yep, It's not the first time she's been injured in the line of duty so I'm not surprised that the incident hasn't dented or weakened her desire to continue in police work. I've suggested to her in the past that she should transfer to training but she isn't interested, she obviously wants to be where the action is hottest. Looks like she got a little more than she bargained for, maybe she'll slow down a little."

Linc takes a deep sigh when he finishes speaking and stands up and walks to the window to look outside. He stands silent for a minute or so before coming back to sit beside me on the bed again. A couple of seconds later Dr. Hill walks in.

"Hi guys. Hey Sydney I hear you've been jogging up and down the hallways." He remarks.

"Not quite doctor, at least not yet. I'm feeling pretty good though." I reply.

"Good, good. Your bleeding has reduced in volume and apparently you haven't had any cramps in the last 48 hours, right?"

"Yes, but I'll be glad when these babies are finally out."

"Patience young lady, all in good time. I just saw one of the ladies down the hall and thought I'd come round to see you too. It's a flying visit, however I'll see you tomorrow morning, okay?"

"Of course. I take it you won't be here all day tomorrow or will you?"

"I'll work till about noon then I'll head home for some turkey." Dr. Hill replies.

"Lucky you Doc. see you tomorrow then."

Dr. Hill shakes hands with Linc and leaves. Linc and I spend a while talking about Omar. Apparently he had returned to Los Angeles but from the way things stood with him, he might return any day. No one knows where Kephern is; maybe he's still in New York. I don't really care and I'm not bothered either. Even though we talked about Omar and Kephern, I notice that I am doing most of the talking. Linc is mostly silent, just making a few grunts and comments here and there. The expression on his face belies whatever he is really thinking. I didn't blame him for hitting Omar but whenever

I thought about it I'm still kinda surprised. Even though I know how fit Linc is and how he feels he can take care of himself, I hadn't thought I'd actually see him get violent. Oh well, maybe it was for the better and if Omar does come back, I hope Ricky or someone is around to put out any sparks. With the two of them in the room together the other day, I'd felt like I was between a rock and a hard place. Who knows, if they ever did meet again it could be civil.

CHAPTER 27
SYDNEY COLLINS-CALDWELL/ LINCOLN CALDWELL

Friday January 2nd
Manhattan, NY

Christmas has come and gone, I've had two close calls so far re: my babies, including the one this morning and here I am. Still in bed and still attached to this contraption that I wheel around on my walks. I'd even gotten into trouble two days ago when I pulled the syringe out of my wrist and got onto the elevator to the ground floor to get some exercise. Talk about nearly causing a panic. This morning however had scared even me. For some reason I'd woken up with blood all over the sheets again and I'd pressed the red panic button. The nurses and the doctor on duty had rushed me into the theatre, fully prepared to perform a caesarian on me. All of them had been sure that the time had come, that the babies were coming out. There had also been some fetal distress registering on the baby monitor. Thankfully the erratic fetal heartbeats had subsided and the bleeding had stopped. I'd been given some medication and a couple of injections and then I had been taken back to my room. I still feel quite strong but I am definitely impatient and fed up of being in hospital. I have been here about five weeks and that's a very *long* time. My eyes have been closed for the past few minutes but of course I could hear everyone around me. Mama is here as well as Dad, Ryoko, Pastor Al and Pastor Vince. They had all arrived within ten minutes of each other. I had been standing at my window trying to see if I could see Linc in the car park. I also spent long moments wishing I could get out there and walk in the snow, maybe even lie on my back and move my arms and legs to form an angel in the snow. I would even love to feel the cold biting wind on my face. Snow always fascinates me, the way it will sit beautifully on trees and flowers and buildings and even on people's clothing as they walked along the streets. But at the same time it looks messy as it forms black sludge on the streets as cars drive by.

"So when are Ricky and Khreeo getting back from Hawaii Linc?" I hear Dad ask.

"Day after tomorrow sir."

"Valerie, I think we should go to Hawaii soon, we'll be able to get some of the stuff you've been looking for." Dad adds.

"Uh huh honey we'll plan it as soon as we get back to Boston." Ma replies.

Pastors Vince and Al have been here for over 30 minutes and I can see they are ready to leave.

"Pastor Vince when will I get to speak to you again? and thank you for the advice on Omar."

"Don't worry about him, he's not a problem, besides I know you and Linc have things in order and always remember to look heavenward for help. Give me a call anytime, you've got my numbers right?"

"Yes I have all your numbers and Pastor Al's too. Thank you both for coming to see me."

Pastor Al smiles as he stands up to leave and Pastor Vince shakes my hand. Before leaving the room Pastor Al asks everyone to hold hands while he prayed. Mama gives both pastors a hug as they leave and Linc walks out with them to the elevator.

"I'm glad you've walked with us to the elevator Linc, we've wanted to speak with you without Sydney there."

"I know Pastor Al, Sydney had told me she'd mentioned one or two things to Pastor Vince including her concerns about Ryoko and me." I say.

"Truth is I'm concerned myself. Ryoko and I have maintained a solid relationship since we broke up and it hasn't been a problem for us. While we were dating we had loved each other very much but our relationship had been quite tumultuous. We both concluded afterward that we make much better friends than lovers. Before Sydney came along we continued doing most things together. If we weren't in the company of the rest of the 'gang' we were with each other. At the movies, theatre, park, gym, my motorcycle rides and even when I'm painting, we were almost always together. She has no family here and during low times or emotional distressing times at work we'd comfort each other. Whenever I was down we would speak on the phone for hours at a time. But even though we paid all this attention to one another we both accepted the fact that we were just good buddies. We hug very regularly, I'll kiss her on the forehead or cheek whenever we meet or part but that is it."

I go silent for a second, take a deep breath and continue.

"My worry now is that it seems the feelings have escalated a little since this life threatening incident she went through."

"Whose feelings have escalated Linc, yours or hers?" asks Pastor Al.

"In all honesty I think both of us. I didn't think I had a choice in spending all that time with her in hospital before she was discharged. *She did almost die*! I am the only person she kept asking for when she came through her operation. We've both said at various times over the past few years that we love each other but it has always been said with the understanding of caring love not erotic. However this last couple of weeks has been slightly different. I held her hand one in day in hospital and I just felt different and it has felt different ever since. When we look at each other now there is certain guilt in both our eyes and we're both afraid that Sydney or any one of our other friends may notice. We haven't done anything but we both know that for some reason there's been a subtle change. To make matters worse Sydney and Ryoko have always liked each other so you can see…….

The pastors and I step into the elevator without saying a word and no one speaks for the duration of the ride down to the ground floor. As the doors re-opens on the ground floor Pastor Vince is the first to speak.

"You are an intelligent man Linc; you're also wise enough to know what to do in this situation. I will not proceed to insult you by stating the obvious. However what I will say is that in relation to affairs of the heart even adults don't always behave rationally. You and Ryoko cannot leave things the way they are now…hanging in the air, you've got to put an end to what could potentially cause disaster. I really don't see Ryoko wanting to hurt Sydney intentionally but again, when it comes to affairs of the heart people can be selfish and throw all caution to the wind. Remember the 'world' says 'all's fair in love and war' throughout your courtship and so far in your marriage you and Ryoko have kept your relationship platonic, unfortunately you may now find that a little more difficult. You believe in God so you know everything is possible if you put it in prayer. Have a sit down with Ryoko and deal with it. Your wife doesn't need to know about it just yet. There is no telling how she could react and in her current state of health, *that* is an important consideration."

"I will do that, in fact it's what I had been thinking of doing anyway. I'll speak with you and let you know how it all goes. Thanks."

By this time we have arrived at the car. I shake hands with them and stand and watch them drive out of the hospital parking lot. It seems I have my work cut out for me over the next 24 hours. I turn around and walk back through the hospital lobby.

CHAPTER 28
SYDNEY COLLINS-CALDWELL

Sunday January 11th
Manhattan, NY

I glance at my watch, 11a.m. Ironic, I'm thinking. I'm being rushed to the delivery room again, this time I have a feeling it's for real. I muse at the fact that it's 11a.m on the 11th of January which means that written down it would read 01-11 at 11a.m. I'm fighting to remain calm. I had bled a little earlier on this morning but the real concern is the fetal distress registering on the CTG (Cardiotopograph) machine. About eight minutes ago the nurse had noticed the heartbeats of the babies. They were only around ninety beats per minute and of course everyone is concerned. The immediate response is to get them out. I'm now thirty-four weeks pregnant and the obstetricians are confident of their survival. Dr. Hill has told me that I'm carrying monozygotic twins, so I'm worried that whatever may be causing the abnormal heart beats may affect both of them at the same time. I know that the first part of the procedure includes my being administered with an anesthetic. One of the nurses had mentioned a minute ago that due to the emergency I would be given a general anesthetic, to put me out completely. I'm now being wheeled into the operating room and I squeeze Linc's hand. We've been told that he may not be allowed in to watch the delivery but he seems to be coping very well under the circumstances. I see the nurse gently restrain Linc from coming in, just as the attending doctor inserts a needle into my arm. The doctor explains what he is doing and tells me to count to fifty. I suspect I am not going to reach fifty before I lose consciousness but what the heck, let's see how far I can reach. Here goes, one, two, three, four, five, six...

90 minutes later according to the clock on the wall I finally come round, although Linc tells me later that I'd stepped in and out of consciousness. I feel very groggy but I immediately remember that I

have two babies to ask after. I try to speak and raise my head off the pillows but no sound comes out of my mouth and I'm too weak or tired to move. Thankfully Linc is there to assist me. I can also see a nurse, a doctor and Lola. I look around the room, but I can't see any baby cots. Oh yes, I remember the doctors had said something about them going into an incubator due to them being premature.

"Hello sweetheart, how are you feeling?" Linc asks.

"A little groggy Linc, where are my babies?"

Rather than answer me directly, I see him glance over at the doctor first. I suddenly feel physically sick and I almost lose consciousness again. If I hadn't already been so weak I'm sure I'd have screamed at everyone in the room.

"What is it Linc? Answer me ……."

I'm trying to shout but all I can muster is a weak, hoarse, semi-whisper. My throat has gone dry. "For the love of God… someone tell me something." I continue.

Everyone of course is now gathered around my bed and I can see concern and anguish on Linc's face and in his eyes. Lola also looks grieved and I can see she has been crying. Linc takes both my hands in his and tries to speak but he too can't. Try as he must be, he can't stop himself from bursting and that is the last straw for me. I begin flailing my arms around and tossing and turning in the bed. I know something is terribly wrong and I can only guess that my babies are abnormal or worse still, dead! Lola and the nurse are trying to calm me down and through my tears I can see and hear that Linc has totally lost it. Somebody had better tell me something because I am beginning to lose my mind. The doctor comes over and stands by my bedside. He props me up on my pillows and begins to speak.

"Mrs. Caldwell, I'm Dr Rhodes, I'm your attending Neonatologist. I have some good news and some bad news relating of course to your twins. I'm really very sorry to tell you that it's not all good news as obviously expected. The good news is….one of your babies is in the Neonatal unit, she's in an incubator being cared for normally and she's doing very well. As you know, your twins were born approximately six weeks early. Although this is an acceptable delivery age, babies this early are usually under-weight and need specialized care. One of your babies was born weighing just 2Ibs 4ozs and the other just over

4lbs 1oz. It's your larger baby that is downstairs in the incubator. She's just one floor below us…"

"Stop!" I manage to splutter.

I feel like dying, I glance at Linc who is now holding my hands again but still looks very drained and nauseous; I hold up one hand for silence and close my eyes for a minute. My mind is racing in all directions one second and then blank the next. I am afraid to hear the rest of what Dr. Rhodes has to say. Something tells me to speak to my Heavenly Father in prayer. I pray silently and I immediately feel my spirit calm. Not that I feel perfectly in control of my emotions especially since I still have some bad news to hear. But I'm now ready to deal with my circumstances and I know that whatever troubles come my way can be overcome with prayer and the love of my husband and family and friends.

"Go ahead doctor."

Dr. Rhodes takes a deep breath and exhales audibly.

"We did all we possibly could but…she was still born and right now we are not yet sure what caused her to be born dead. An autopsy will be conducted in order to discover any possible causes, more likely than not it could be just a lack of oxygen. During the operation to remove them from your womb we saw that her umbilical cord was tight around her neck. We immediately did a heart massage on her but there was no response. We then had to do a DC shock to try and revive her. This too didn't work and unfortunately we had to pronounce her dead almost immediately after. I'm profoundly sorry, no matter how many years of practice we medical staff put in; we are still very distraught when cases like this happen. Please accept my heart felt condolences on behalf of the entire surgical and neonatal staff."

Linc and Lola still haven't said a word during the last ten minutes. He has obviously taken the news very badly maybe even worse than I have. We hug each other and cry. I could faintly hear him mumbling something in my ear over and over again as he weeps. After what seems like an eternity we calm down enough to separate and look at each other. I even manage a wry grin.

"Linc honey, we have a little daughter to look after don't we?"

"Yes sweetheart we do and she's a beauty too. She looks just like you, with big beautiful eyes and tiny dainty little fingers and toes. I looked at her features, her nose, her lips, her ears…she is a stunner already."

"Where is the doctor Linc? I need to know when *I* can see her."

I look around the room only to find out that Doctor Rhodes has left, probably excusing us while we were crying. Lola steps out of the room to get him while Linc and I just hold hands and look into each other's eyes. Dr. Rhodes and another doctor come back into the room. I immediately ask when I could see her.

"You can see her as soon as you feel strong enough. I could have a nurse wheel you in the bed down to the elevator and onto the appropriate floor." Dr. Rhodes responds.

"*I* can do that, I mean wheel her downstairs." Linc offers.

"Sure you can. The nurse will accompany you whenever you're ready. I also want to let you know that we should have the findings from the autopsy by tomorrow morning and we'll keep you informed immediately." He adds.

Linc thanks Dr. Rhodes and he and the other doctor leave the room. I tell Linc I am ready to see my baby.

"Sweetheart, you know we have two names for our babies, which of the two names do you want for her?" Linc asks.

"Teri." I answer

"And let's go see her."

By the time Lola, the nurse, Linc and I reach the elevator we have Dad on the phone with Linc and Woody on the phone with Lola. In addition we could see Ryoko running to catch up with us. Linc holds the doors open till she reaches us and we all huddle together in the elevator as we go down one floor to the Neonatal unit. When we reach the right section of the unit I see about five babies in incubators. The nurse on duty points to the second child as ours and we go over to see her. My first sighting of my baby brings joy to my heart; she looks like a little angel. She is no larger than the palm of Linc's hand. I'm not even put off by the tube attached to her tiny mouth and tiny nose. Linc is absolutely right, she is a stunner, and she even has her shiny black curly hair covering her perfectly shaped head. She looks strawberry creamy and her eyes, even though they are closed, are obviously large. I've fallen in love at first sight and I also feel a sudden pang of sadness as I realize that I could have had two beautiful little angels instead of just one. But I immediately smile as I also realize that I could also have had neither! I again thanked God for his mercies. The nurses tell us that she is doing well and there hasn't been any cause for concern. We all spend the next 20 minutes oooohing and aaaahing over Teri; I hold her tiny hands and touch every inch of her tiny body that isn't wrapped up.

"*This is my baby girl.*" I say out loud, bringing a smile to everyone's face.

CHAPTER 29
SYDNEY COLLINS-CALDWELL

Friday January 16th
Manhattan, NY

"Hi girl, it's Sydney what's up?"

"Heya Sydney. I'm really sorry I haven't gotten to New York yet. I just haven't been able to get time off from work. My boss is really being hard-nosed about it. I still hope though that I'll be able to get away real soon. How are you anyway? Really! And little Teri?"

"She's great Tiffany, putting on weight and doing all the normal baby things, eating, sleeping etc. Thank goodness for the weekly injections I used to get to strengthen the babies' lungs. I didn't look forward to them because they were extremely painful, I always felt like I was being kicked in the leg by a mule. The doctors have also been pleased with her progress so far and of course we're all happy. Listen Tiffany I can't stay long on the phone I just want to let you know that we're all fine. I'm waiting for you to come visit so keep working on your boss okay?"

"Sure thing girl, I'll give you a call tomorrow, don't worry I'll be there soon."

"Good. I'll speak to you tomorrow then, bye....."

I hang up and glance at the doorway. Mama and Carla walk into the room together. Carla comes over to me while Mama starts to speak with Lynn and Linc who are also in the room. I glance at my bedside clock 1.23p.m I'm feeling sleepy again. Even though I realize I'm a long way from getting all my strength and energy back, I still get a little irritated with myself for feeling sleepy and weak most of the day. Both Dr. Rhodes and Dr. Hill have explained to me that a caesarian is a major operation and I should allow myself ample time to heal. I close my eyes and listen to the familiar hum of voices around me. I feel at peace, I have a loving husband, a daughter, loving parents and very good friends. They have all contributed to my being able to cope with the tragedy of losing one of my twins. The autopsy had come back confirming what Dr. Rhodes had initially suspected. She had died from asphyxiation; her oxygen supply had been cut off by the umbilical cord that had somehow wrapped around her neck. Exactly how and why it happened, I'll never know. What I do know is that she went straight back to heaven as innocent and angelic as she had arrived. My sadness has also been alleviated because I still have Teri.

I can hear Lynn cracking some joke and Carla and Ricky laughing. Linc says something about not knowing his sister had joined Carla's profession as a comedian. I open my eyes briefly and see Ricky and Khreeo holding each other tightly. I'm glad for them; it seems they have really fallen in love. Over the past couple of months they've been practically inseparable. Khreeo has actually moved to New York and has been lackadaisically looking for employment, so when Ricky is at work she's had a lot of time on her hands and that's one of the reasons I've seen her everyday, except when they were in Hawaii. Ricky has been trying to convince her to move in with him but so far she's been able to resist. She's currently living with an aunt of hers in Long Island but I suspect her resolve is being eroded slowly but surely. Linc and I are pretty certain she'll move in with Ricky shortly. Khreeo had told me yesterday that she'll be going to the Czech Republic with Ricky next month for a chess tournament he's playing in. She's very excited about the planned trip and can't wait to get to see Europe. I recall smiling when she had told me, because not only has she taken up playing chess but is turning out to be quite good, she even reads and studies some of Ricky's chess books.

Pastor Vince had stopped by on Monday and we had gone to see Teri downstairs. He had prayed over her extensively and we'd sat and talked for a while downstairs before he left. The only annoyance I've felt over the past few days was when Omar had called. He had extended his condolences and his congratulations but had spoilt it by adding he was coming to New York to see me. Of course I discouraged him fervently, I told him I never wanted to see him again, in fact I didn't even want him to call me either. But of course he had been his normal stubborn self, now I'm concerned about whenever he does show up because I haven't told Linc. I sigh audibly and suddenly realize that the whole room has gone silent.

"Are you okay sweetheart?" asks my husband.

"You seem bothered about something."

"I'm fine honey, don't mind me I was just lost in thought."

"What were you thinking about?" Mama queries.

"Nothing much Ma, don't worry about it, I'm fine, honest."

"Okay if you insist." She adds with a raised eyebrow.

I know that she hasn't believed me but she can't press any further. I decide to get into the conversations before someone else decides to probe.

"Hey Lynn how's Atlanta?"

She clicks her lips and tongue in that way African and Caribbean women do (I've always wanted to ask her how she does that) and then replies.

"What kind of question is that girl? You know the ATL is always slamming! There's something going on out there all the time nowadays and we've now got almost as many celebrities living there as here in New York!"

"Yeh right Lynn. I see you're still campaigning to get Linc and I to move out there, aren't you?"

Everybody laughs except Mama, who as usual doesn't have much of a sense of humor. Anyway Lynn says she hasn't given up on her quest and adds that Linc would only be coming home. A nurse walks in to announce that Kephern is at the nurses' station; do I want to see him? I look at Linc quizzically and he shrugs his shoulders. I tell the nurse to let him through. A few moments later he walks into the room.

"Hi everyone, hi Syd how are you?"

There is a long pause before I answer. I'm really not sure how to receive him. No one currently in the room including Mama is impressed with the stunt he and Omar had pulled a couple of weeks ago. Needless to say the both of them are still in Linc's worst books. My pause must have been too long because Mama decides to speak first.

"I hope you intend to behave yourself young man and that you've brought your good manners along with you today." She says.

"Yes ma'am." Kephern replies.

I decide it is time for me to speak to the man; after all it is me he's come to see.

"Hello Kephern ……we're fine, that is Teri and I. And she's getting bigger and stronger every day. How about you though? How's work?"

"Work is fine Syd. Here, I brought some gifts for you and the baby, I hope you like them."

He hands over a bag he has carried in with him. It contains a bunch of baby clothes and some baby shoes too. I thank him and he then informs everyone that he has to leave. He spends a couple more minutes speaking with Carla and then leaves. Mama is next to inform me she is leaving. She has to get back to her hotel to conduct some last minute business with a client. Both Linc and I have told her to move out of the hotel and stay at our house but she has refused, saying she doesn't want to get in the way. However she did say she'll consider spending at least a couple of nights with us before going back to Boston. I on the other hand am anxious to get back into my own bed. The past six weeks in this hospital bed is definitely more than enough for me. The doctors have told me I should be discharged within ten days of delivery, which means by next Wednesday. Unfortunately they did warn me that Teri might not be discharged for a while after. They also add that Teri might not actually be in hospital for as long as originally estimated.

By 5p.m everyone has left, including Linc. I take a nap for an hour and I am woken up at 6p.m by Tiffany calling from Madrid. We spend an hour and a half gisting before she rings off. I call Linc at home and Ma at the hotel. By the time I am through with all my telephone conversations I am tired again. I decide to call it a night and I turn out the bedside lamp and fall asleep.

CHAPTER 30
SYDNEY COLLINS-CALDWELL

**Tuesday January 20th
Manhattan, NY**

I swing my legs out of bed and get up. I bend over my baby's cot, pick her up, kiss her and walk over to the window. I look out at the falling white snowflakes and the snow-covered rooftops. I'm still looking forward to stepping out of the hospital into the cold winter breeze. Having lived in Boston most of my life I'm familiar with and sometimes even look forward to cold weather. There is a knock on the door. It is Dr. Rhodes.

"Good afternoon Mrs. Caldwell, how are you and baby Teri?"

"Fine, I just woke up a few minutes ago and she's still sleeping in my arms here." I say looking down at Teri.

"Great, well I'll only be a second or two with her. Would you place her on her back in her cot please?"

I lay Teri down as instructed and watch as Dr. Rhodes examines her. It is a daily routine that I've grown accustomed to. Every morning a doctor would stop by on his or her ward round. Most of the time it has been Dr. Rhodes so I'm not surprised to see him again this morning. I notice that he has creased his eyebrows in a kind of frown.

"What's the matter doctor?" I ask apprehensively.

"Just one moment Mrs. Caldwell." He replies, while continuing his examination for a few moments more.

"Did you notice that she's running a high temperature Mrs. Caldwell?"

"No I didn't actually. I haven't touched her other than to give her a light kiss on her forehead when I picked her up. I didn't notice anything wrong."

"She does have a high fever and from my observation here it seems she may also have an enlarged spleen and liver. I'll have to run some tests immediately."

This is bad, I think to myself. I've prayed all morning and into this afternoon. God can't let me down now, can He? I've been battling and feel I'm doing well with handling my loss of just nine days ago.

How can this be happening? Linc is in a mess; he'd arrived some hours ago when I had called him in a panic. He'd stayed here till a few minutes ago and had had to leave for an appointment. Mama is here, sitting next to my bed and Khreeo is down the hall speaking to Ricky on her cell phone. Teri has gotten worse, she has developed a skin rash and her eyes are kind of light yellow. Her fever has been kind of undulating and the soft spot on her head (fontanel) is bulging out abnormally. In addition she's become floppy. The doctor had lifted her arms and legs and they had just flopped back down, he'd called it hypotonia or something. Her yellowy eyes mean she's probably jaundiced. They have taken nearly 2mls. of blood from her for various blood tests and I'm anxiously waiting for the results.

Khreeo and Mama are arguing about something as I wake up. The nurse had given me a sedative of some sort earlier on because I'd been in bad shape. I think I'd fallen asleep around 4p.m and right now I have no idea what the time is.

"Mama, what time is it. Have the blood test results come back yet?"

"You're awake Sydney?"

"Of course I'm awake Ma……well?" I ask impatiently.

I see Mama curl up the corner of her mouth in indignation at how I had just spoken to her. But I can't be bothered about that.

"No they have not. I'm sure they'll get them to us any minute now and by the way the time is 6.20p.m."

6.20p.m! How had I been able to sleep for more than two hours? I couldn't believe it; whatever the nurse had given me had certainly worked well. Even when I'd taken the medicine I'd thought 'Yeah right' this isn't going to work.

Fifteen minutes later Ryoko and Linc arrive together. How had they linked up? I thought. I take a deep breath and decide to dismiss it, at least temporarily. Linc helps me out of bed. I need to move around a bit. Ryoko doesn't say anything; she smiles at me and gives me a little wave as she sits next to Khreeo.

"Hi sweetheart, I bumped into Dr. Rhodes in the elevator, he'll be here any second." Linc offers.

A full thirty minutes pass before Dr. Rhodes did come in.

"Hello everybody." He says rather solemnly.

"Mr. And Mrs. Caldwell, I'm sorry I have some more disturbing news for you."

I get back into bed and try to calm myself down, my heart racing and my head suddenly pounding again. Dr. Rhodes continues.

"The lab results of the blood tests show that your baby has hypertrigly ceridaemia, which simply means she has too much fat or cholesterol in her blood. Furthermore she has cytopenia, which is an immune system derangement. In other words she has little or no white blood cells for immunity against diseases and or abnormally low blood platelets used for blood clotting. Her red blood cells are also too low. We are conducting further tests even as we speak. I'm quite puzzled over these results and I'll be consulting with the senior pediatrician later on today."

"What does all this mean?" Linc asks.

"Well, at this time we're not 100% sure. I'll be able to give a more accurate diagnosis after we get the further results and after speaking with the senior pediatrician. I think you should remain as calm as possible, we're doing all that we can right now. Your baby will be fine okay?"

I nod weakly, Linc has a blank look on his face and I couldn't look at him for more than a second or two.

"Heavenly Father…." I call out loudly.

"I know you haven't abandoned me…..but where are you in all this? Save my baby, heal my baby I want her healthy and strong."

I start to cry again, Ryoko and Khreeo come over and hug me. I'm not sure I can cope with all this; it's getting too much to bear. I have to speak to my Dad.

CHAPTER 31
SYDNEY COLLINS-CALDWELL

Wednesday January 21st
Manhattan, NY

I have no idea why Linc isn't here yet or why he hasn't called either. Dr. Rhodes had popped in for a few seconds only to tell me he'll be back very soon. All he said was that the results are in and that he's spoken to the senior pediatrician. There is no one in the room with me at the moment, I feel kind of lonely. I can hear some one coming toward my room, it's probably the doctor……..it is.

"Good morning again Mrs. Caldwell, I know you have been anxious so I'll get right down to it."

He pulls up a chair and sits down.

"What I'm about to tell you may sound rather drastic and confusing but I'll do my best to simplify it as much as possible. The blood test shows cytotoxicity, which means that her T-cells are dying. Your baby has little or no natural killer cells. This condition is uncommon and when I spoke to Dr. Williamson he was puzzled too. He went on to inform me about a finding in a recent medical journal he had read. There is an under diagnosed condition called FHL (Familial Hemophagocytic Lymphohistiocytosis) which on a hunch based on all the blood test results from your baby, he has prompted me to pursue. In order to proceed I will need to do a genetic study on both parents and baby so I'll be needing blood samples from both you and Mr. Caldwell. Cytotoxicity combined with the other findings in your baby's condition is a striking finding in FHL and because it is an under diagnosed condition, I feel we should pursue it quickly. First of all we have to begin immediate treatment for your baby, which means chemotherapy. After the chemotherapy course of treatment is exhausted we will then have to do a BMT (Bone Marrow Transplant) to ultimately cure her, so we'll be doing a bone marrow examination.

The results of the bone marrow examination take 1 day for the first result and a week for the second."

I am stunned ……cytotoxicity, lympho…, chemotherapy, surely he can't be talking about *my* baby! And a bone marrow transplant? How is Linc going to take this? I've found out in the last week or so that I'm much stronger than Linc emotionally. He hasn't handled any of what happened well. The death of one of our babies and all this negative information has seemingly crushed him. I'm actually a little concerned about him and angry too. I'd always thought that my husband would support and strengthen me emotionally not the other way round. But I know that you learn more and more about a person as time goes on. I've certainly discovered I'm stronger than I've ever imagined, I think motherhood is going to suit me just fine.

"What is this FHL exactly?" I ask the doctor.

"It is an anomaly that I myself am going to read and study up on. Dr. Williamson is going to consult with me on the issue, so I'll give you more information very soon. When will your husband be here?"

"He should be here soon; I'll let the nurse know so that she can inform you right away. I know you need the blood samples immediately."

Linc doesn't arrive till late afternoon and again he shows up with Ryoko. This time I'm not able to hold back, I've been waiting for him all day long and so I lay into him angrily.

"Where the h… have you been? And what are *you* doing here Ryoko? You've been able to grab my husband from me at every opportunity, I'm sick of it. I don't want you here; don't come to see me ever again. *Do you hear me?*" I scream.

I must have been shouting very loudly because a couple of nurses come running into the room. I'm sure the hospital has nicknamed my room the 'drama room' by now. There always seems to be excitement in here.

"Mrs. Caldwell are you alright?" one of them asks.

"No I'm not. I want this woman to leave, get her out of here!"

The nurses and Linc usher Ryoko out of the room and because he didn't come back in immediately I continued to fume. He spends a couple of minutes placating Ryoko and by the time he did come back in to speak with me I was ready to lambast him again.

"What exactly is wrong with you Linc? Do you want Ryoko?" I shout.

"Calm down Sydney I…"

"Don't tell me to calm down." I scream again.

Linc lifts his arms in surrender; he shrugs his shoulders and sits down at the foot of my bed in silence. With him silent my rage falls silent as well. We both sit here for what seems like an eternity.

"Dr. Williamson and Dr. Rhodes need our blood for some tests." I finally say.

I proceed to tell him of all that the doctors had told me about Teri's condition. He sits in total silence all through. When I finally finish my narration I look at him expectantly, waiting for a response. I press the buzzer for the nurse, when she comes I tell her to inform Dr. Rhodes that my husband is here.

Dr. Rhodes and a nurse arrive shortly afterward. I explain to him that I've told Linc about the situation. The nurse takes blood from both Linc and I then leaves. Dr. Rhodes on the other hand stays and talks to us for ten minutes. He again tells us that within 24 hours we would have the first results of Teri's bone marrow examination and the second in a week. He goes on to give us a long monologue of medical terminology that we can't grasp, at the end of it all he had to explain in plain English. What it boils down to is that our daughter has a condition that is rare and fatal if not caught early. In a way we are lucky that she has presented certain symptoms and that Dr. Williamson had been aware of what those symptoms could possibly mean. The most shocking thing he did say however is that the FHL condition only tends to present itself in children that are offspring of closely related parents! We both told him that *that certainly* isn't the case with us. There is no way we could be related. He eventually leaves us with our thoughts and trepidations. In my opinion the only things left for us to do are look after Teri and pray.

I suddenly remember that I haven't seen my baby for a few hours, so I get up.

"I'm going to see *our baby*, you coming?" I ask Linc.

45 minutes later we return to my room. Teri is asleep for the entire 45minutes. I had written a new poem yesterday to take my mind off things. And because writing poems relaxes me, I'll try and write another one. Mama and the rest of the 'gang' show up and we spend the rest of the evening looking somber whilst trying to fake high spirits.

CHAPTER 32
SYDNEY COLLINS-CALDWELL

Thursday January 29th
Manhattan, NY

I have now come to accept the fact that I may have a lifetime of careful care to administer to Teri. Her condition, in addition to being rare is also very care intensive. I haven't seen Linc since yesterday morning, more than 24 hours ago. I had spoken to him briefly last night and he's supposed to be here straight from work. It's nearly 8 p.m now and he still hasn't shown up. Since last week when we'd had the big row over Ryoko and I'd shouted at her and had her walked out of my room, Linc and I have stayed on pretty bad terms. My mood has mostly remained somber and angry not to mention concerned and apprehensive in regards to Teri's condition. She has fallen in and out of relatively good days and bad days. The chemotherapy treatment seems to be going pretty well and she has responded positively. My little baby does seem to be a fighter!

I have called both Ricky and Woody but neither of them have seen or heard from Linc all day. I have also tried to reach him on his cell phone but to no avail.

"Hello Mrs. Caldwell."

It's Dr. Rhodes as he walks through the door.

"Is your husband around? I have the results of your tests." He continues.

"And I think it might be best if I could speak with the two of you together."

"I haven't spoken with him since last night doctor; he'll probably show up any second. Why do we have to wait for him anyway? I've been waiting for these results all week."

"I have very sensitive information for the two of you; I think it'll be better for you guys to hear it together."

I put my hand up for Dr. Rhodes to give me a moment while I pick up my cell phone again to try Linc once more. The phone rings and rings and I eventually cut it off. I then try Woody and Lola's house.

"Hi Woody it's me, any word from Linc? I'm still waiting for him."

"No Sydney and neither has Lola. I'm quite surprised and a little worried too."

We speak for just another minute before I ring off. I put the phone back down on my bedside table and looked over at Dr. Rhodes. I shrug my shoulders and raise my eyebrows quizzically.

"What now doctor?" I ask.

"Tell you what Mrs. Caldwell. I'll go see my other patients and be back in an hour or so, how about that?"

"Okay doctor, I'll see you then. Hopefully he'll be here."

After Dr. Rhodes leaves the room I again begin to reflect on the events of the past few weeks. This must be the one-hundredth time I'll do so but there are so many things happening with my life that I really have no choice but to reflect.

A little over an hour later Dr. Rhodes comes back into my room. Linc had arrived 30 minutes earlier and Woody and Lola had just knocked on my door a few moments before the doctor. Lola is in the early stages of berating Linc over where he had disappeared to when the doctor walks in, so she's had to stop temporarily. I can see her face and eyes are still screwed up in annoyance. Surprisingly I haven't said much to Linc since he has shown up. He has offered some excuses or the other but I haven't really paid much attention to what he has said. I am too apprehensive and expectant about what Dr. Rhodes has to say, so I couldn't really concentrate on anything else. The only thing I have questioned Linc on is why he's looking a little disheveled. Normally he is always either smartly dressed in his casual smart type clothing, like in a nice shirt and casual dress pants and nice loafers or he'll be in a suit for work, or still look dapper in a pair of jeans, t-shirt and sport jacket. Today however, he has on a pair of his old blue jogging pants which have a rip on the left leg, an old pair of dirty blue and white running Reebok trainers on his feet, a white t-shirt underneath a gray sweater, and he hasn't shaved either! I actually asked him whether he has been running in the snow!

"Well, Mr. And Mrs. Caldwell are you ready for the results?"

It is Dr. Rhodes cutting through my reverie. Before either Linc or I could respond he holds up both hands, turns to Woody and Lola and says...

"As I mentioned earlier to Mrs. Caldwell this information is rather sensitive, so if you wouldn't mind excusing us...."

"Not a problem doctor, my wife and I will go get some coffee down the hall. Let us know when you're through." Woody answers.

With that, Lola gives me a quick peck on my cheek while whispering

"Be strong sweetheart." She smiles and she and Woody walk out.

I settle into my bed as best I can, try to calm myself down and glance over at Linc who in my opinion is looking lost. He has refused to sit since he came into the room more than half an hour ago. As upset as I am with him before he had arrived I also feel concerned. He isn't behaving like the Linc I've known and the only obvious reason is that he's handling the events of my being in hospital the last seven or so weeks, our baby's death and our other baby's illness, very badly. My jumping down his throat recently regarding Ryoko hasn't helped either but hers is an issue that needs to be dealt with regardless of my current circumstances. As things stand now I have just decided to deal with this bigger issue re: Teri and seek the best way forward over her care and well being. I love my husband but I also realize he's an adult and should be able to take care of himself, unlike Teri who needs all my attention. And for that matter, needs her father's attention too. So it seems I'll have to call Linc to order on that score also! I take a deep breath just as Linc does too, glance over at Dr. Rhodes, give him a wry smile and say...

"Go right ahead doctor..."

Dr. Hill asks Linc to sit but he refuses.

"There's only one way to say this to you both…the blood samples when ran for DNA testing shows that you are related to each other. In fact, closely related…we ran this particular test three times with the same results. It is irrefutable; Mrs. Caldwell the crux of the matter is that Mr. Caldwell is your *father!*

There is stunned silence in the room for what seems like an eternity. Then Linc speaks.

"That is impossible…impossible, absolutely impossible." He repeats in a choked voice.

"I'm afraid there is no mistake Mr. Caldwell. Believe me, this is as unusual and surprising to us as it is to you. Our suspicions that there is a relationship between the two of you were initially aroused as a result of your baby's condition." Dr. Rhodes continues.

"Of course we have no idea how the circumstance came about and my first impression is that even the two of you have no clue as to how you got to this point. The FHL findings as mentioned earlier are an indicator and although rare it has happened before at this hospital. I'd like to give you some information on these topics…consanguinity and consanguineous relationships and then you both should undergo some genetic counseling."

Both Linc and I are still in stunned silence, so Dr. Rhodes continues.

"Those two terms I just mentioned are words that are not readily understood by the average person, they are certainly not used as part of everyday vocabulary, even in the medical field. I've written down some notes to help me explain the situation to you in layman's terms. Firstly a marriage is said to be consanguineous when the union is between two people genetically related. That of course covers brother and sister, father and daughter, mother and son and even cousins. Many first cousins however are married to each other around the world. In fact studies have shown that 20% of the world's married couples are first cousins to each other. Even many famous people married their first cousins, for example; Albert Einstein and Charles Darwin. President Roosevelt married his cousin of the same last name but she wasn't his first cousin though. The first Prime Minister of Canada, Sir John Macdonald was also married to his first cousin. I have a quote here from Darwin from way back in 1871. He said and I quote 'When the principles of breeding and of inheritance are better understood, we shall not hear ignorant members of our legislature rejecting with scorn, a plan for ascertaining by an easy method whether or not consanguineous marriages are injurious to man.' End quote. Obviously cousins have been falling in love and getting married for centuries. In fact no European country prohibits marriages between first cousins. The frequency of cousin relationships in the United States is 1 in 1000. In Japan for instance it's 4 in 1000. However in other nations especially in the Middle East it's even more prevalent. In Saudi Arabia consanguinity is 34% to 80%! I know the cousin relationships I have quoted statistics on are not the same as your situation but I just thought maybe the information might help in some way. I also know that you are both Christians so I took particular note of something I came across in the medical journals on this subject. In the bible Leviticus 18 lists all forbidden sexual relationships; cousin relationships are not included on that list. It seems that God even ordered cousin marriages in the bible. If I'm not mistaken God told Abraham to marry Sarah and this is despite the fact that she was his half-sister!"

He pauses for a moment to look at Linc and I. It seems he wants to make sure we haven't lost it. He asks permission to continue and when neither of us responds he surges ahead anyway.

"Children of non-related parents have a 2-3% risk of birth defects but children of first cousins have only a slightly higher risk at 4-6%. All in all birth defects occur under many different circumstances, whether or not a set of parents are related is only one possible reason. Never the less certain ailments and contra-indications that present themselves in new born or infants may indicate and alert modern medical practitioners to the possibility of a consanguineous relationship between the parents, which is what happened in your case. A previous similar case I was involved in at this hospital a year ago, had two infants presenting with opthalmoplegia and severe myopia. These conditions themselves are not necessarily rare but together and in persons so young aroused suspicions of consanguinity."

There is a knock on my door. I can see Woody and Lola as they poke their heads round the slightly ajar door.

"Are you guys through yet?" Woody asks.

"Just about, I'm about to leave Mr. and Mrs. Caldwell to their thoughts and investigations. I'm sure they have a lot to discuss."

Dr. Rhodes makes his excuses and leaves. I still don't have anything to say and apparently neither does Linc. The silence and tension in the room hang so thick that even our visitors fall silent. I fully understand what the doctor had narrated but Linc couldn't be my father, maybe a cousin. Or could he? I try to recall every detail that mama had told me over the years about my relatives. She had fought tooth and nail to remove herself from her family background and history. I've known for a long time that I have a first cousin whom I've never met. He's my mother's sister's son. Could that cousin be Linc? It can't be though…my aunt is younger than my mother so she can't possibly be Linc's mother; she isn't old enough. I have to get hold of Mama tonight no matter how late. Linc is still at the window lost in his own thoughts. I swing my legs out of bed with the intention of crossing the room to Linc. Just as I take my first step toward him he turns, looks at me, Woody and Lola and without a word practically runs out of the room.

Suddenly the strength drains out of my legs and I collapse into Woody's arms. Where am I going to get my strength and solace? My husband seems to be unable or incapable of providing them for me at this time. From the Lord…that's where my help comes from and my solace. What I need to do now is call Mama.

"Whatever information you were just given must have been seriously heavy." says Lola.

"Yep." agrees her husband.

My phone begins to ring….

"Hello is that Mrs. Caldwell?"

"No it's not but hang on a minute, I'll see if she can talk right now." answers Lola.

I take the call from Lola.

"Hello." I manage weakly.

"It's Dr. Hill. Long time no see or speak. I hear some unusual things have occurred since I last saw you and your husband. Could I see you tomorrow some time?" he asks.

"Sure. It'll be nice to see you again. There are a million questions I have for you; maybe you'll be able to clear my head for me. I'll look forward to seeing you then. Thanks." I reply.

I hang up the phone and slump onto my bed fully prepared to just sleep and sleep, so that I could escape my thoughts. Lola and Woody are strenuously trying to get me to tell them what is going on. I tell them I have to call my parents but since they would be in the room listening to the conversation, I might as well give them the information first hand. I spent the next 20 minutes updating Woody and Lola. I tell them all that Dr. Rhodes had said. I also go on to tell them about what I myself had read on the Internet a couple of days ago in the hospital study/lounge. The little I had read up on the Internet about consanguinity alerted me to the fact that there is a higher risk of congenital and familial diseases such as cardiac defects, congenital dislocation of the hip, blindness, asthma and diabetes. I had read that in some parts of the world especially in Pakistan and in Jordan, infant mortality and stillbirths, thalassaemia and a disease called Kufor-Rakeb were prevalent, the latter rendering the victims bed bound and dependent on their families from their teenage years. What have I done to my baby and myself?   I dial Mama at home from my cell phone but there is no response. I try again, this time I call her cell phone.

"Hello Ma." I say as she answers.

"Hello dear, how are you and Teri?"

"Mama I need you to tell me the truth and I need you to tell me now. Who and where is my biological father?"

There is silence from the other side of the line; obviously I've caught her unawares. I give her no more time to ponder over the answer she wants to give me plus I am getting angry.

"You heard me Mama, well? All my life you've given me one story or another, this time I want the truth."

"I think your father is dead." She finally answers.

"I haven't seen or heard from him since before you were born. Why this sudden interest anyway?"

"You're lying to me Mama." I scream down the phone at her.

"If you don't tell me the truth right now I'll make sure you never see me or Teri again. *Do you hear me Mama?*"

Again there is silence on the phone. Woody and Lola are trying to calm me down and Lola actually takes the phone from me and speaks to Mama.

"Good evening Valerie, this is Lola. Sydney's going through some very disturbing circumstances right now; I think she needs to hear you come clean on this issue. When you find out what has happened you'll understand why she's so upset."

"I appreciate your concern Lola but I don't need you to speak on behalf of my daughter, besides it is none of your business. Put Sydney back on the line."

Lola hands the phone back to me with a disgusted look on her face.

"Yes Mama...."

"Your father will be back shortly, we'll both get on the plane as soon as possible, most likely tomorrow and we'll fly to New York to speak to you in person, okay?"

"Alright Mama but for my sanity's sake make sure you are here in the morning. Please ask Dad to call me as soon as he gets in. Good night Ma."

Lola tells me how rude Mama had been to her but I am not surprised. At this point I can only hazard many guesses as to what Mama and Dad will tell me tomorrow. Woody tells me they have to leave; it is getting late, 10p.m to be exact. Visiting hours have ended and they have to go to work tomorrow. They promise to check up on Linc on their way home. As worried as I am over Teri and myself I still worry about Linc too. Before they leave we all go round to see Teri. By 10:15p.m Woody and Lola had gone. I get back to my room and switch on my television. The screen is really just a blur of colors and background noises and I really can't concentrate on anything. My cell phone rings but I decide to ignore it until I remember it might be Dad calling. I look at the number display and realize it is he after all.

"Hello Dad I...."

"It's okay honey. Your mother has told me how upset you are. Sorry I couldn't call earlier. I just got in from work. What brought this all up and how are Linc and my grand-daughter?"

"Linc I don't know about, but Teri is doing well, she's getting stronger and will pull through."

"What do you mean by you don't know about Linc? Where is he?"

"He's probably gone home Dad, Linc isn't handling things very well at the moment and I am barely holding on myself. When are you and Mama getting here tomorrow?"

"We should be there with you by noon honey, can you hold on till then? Please do, all will be revealed at that time. Okay?"

"Alright Dad but from what you've just said it means *you* have also been hiding something from me all these years, right?"

"Be patient Sydney, you know I love you dearly and I certainly wouldn't do anything to intentionally harm you. Again, all will be revealed tomorrow."

"Good night Dad, Teri sends her love and kisses too."

CHAPTER 33
LINCOLN CALDWELL

Friday January 30th
Long Island, NY

I'd once heard someone say that not all those who wander are lost. I know exactly what that person means, although in my case there is a twist. I've been wandering all night, driving aimlessly through town for hours. But I'm not lost, at least not geographically however I am lost emotionally. My mind has been doing it's own wandering also, what do I do next? Where do I go from here? What am I to do with myself? I know that the greatest conflict is not between two people but between one person and himself! Looking at the digital clock in my car I see it's 5a.m. I've been parked here, somewhere in long Island for two hours. My cell phone had rang several times over-night, Woody had called three or four times and so had Sydney's dad, Jordan. I have intentionally not answered any of them. On one occasion I had begun to dial Sydney but cut off before it began to ring. What do I even say to her? If what Dr.Rhodes said is true *and* DNA is universally accepted as gospel, then it means I married my daughter! My lovely wife...my daughter? It seems inconceivable! Naturally I have considered what it all means if true. Teri would therefore be both my daughter and my granddaughter; Sydney would be both sister and mother to Teri. How Teri will take this emotionally when she grows up is another issue entirely. What about family and friends and her schoolmates? Would they be cruel and tease her and insult her? Poor child. This is my entire fault! It has to be, after all Valerie must be a drunken one-night stand I obviously must have had while in college. Truth is though, that I've never had a drunken night in my life, I've racked my brain a million times and I cannot recall ever seeing Valerie before the day she and Sydney had shown up at my apartment to see my paintings. Could she have changed in her appearance so much so that I haven't once recognized her in the past few years? I doubted it very much.

I reminisce over my university years in Atlanta. They had been normal. I hadn't really been a Casanova or Don Juan and the few female relationships I'd had, I remember very well. So how is this possible? I feel totally disgusted with the situation and myself. All I ever wanted was a loving woman and it turns out she's my daughter? Damn…what kind of ill luck is that? I can think of only one other possible explanation but that can't be right either. I know that Jordan is actually her adopted father but she's always maintained that Valerie had said her natural father is dead, which indicates that she knows exactly who he is or was! I've never felt more vulnerable than I do now. I don't know where to turn. The first thing I will do though is take a week or more off from work. I have some annual leave I'll use up.

Once again I glance at the clock in the dash, 5:12a.m. I pick up my phone and dial Ryoko.
"Hi Linc…why are you up so early? She answers sleepily.
"I'm in my car on Long Island."
"Long Island? What on earth are you doing there?"
"I was driving around town all night and just happened to end up here. I'm parked in a sub-division, in a cul-de-sac. A number of things have happened since yesterday that has turned my whole world upside down even further."
"Do you want to drive over here? You know you're welcome." Ryoko offers.
"I know. I'm not sure though. First of all I'm so tired I might fall asleep at the wheel."
"No you will not. I'll talk to you while you drive. Otherwise if you sleep in the parked car where you are, the residents will see you when they leave for work in a couple of hours, right?"
I sigh deeply before answering.
"You're right Ryoko but I also don't want to cause any grief for you with Sydney. You know what I mean? I also don't want the other 'gang' members like Lola and Khreeo and maybe even Woody

and Ricky jumping down our throats either. You know what I'm saying?"

"Well it's your call Linc, my doors and windows too for that matter are always open for you." She says with a light chuckle.

I manage a smile before Ryoko continues.

"It's freezing out there Linc, if you won't come here then at least head home. I'll still talk to you to keep you awake. If you do decide to head over here give me 5 minutes notice so I can get some coffee or something stronger ready for you. I could even possibly warm you up another way..." she teases.

I think over my choices for a moment, while looking out the car windshield at the snowflakes, the dim street lights, the nice houses and manicured lawns I can see. There's even a beautiful little yellow and cream ranch style house that hasn't taken down its Christmas lighting yet. I crank the engine put the car into drive and set off. Am I heading to my place, Ryoko's or no place in particular? I haven't decided yet...

"Ryoko, you still there?" I ask.

CHAPTER 34
SYDNEY COLLINS-CALDWELL

Friday January 30th
Manhattan, NY

I hadn't slept much over night. I'd walked around for a while watched television and inevitably run out of things to do. Which leaves me brooding over what Mama might tell me mixed with the fear that what Dr. Rhodes had told Linc and I is true? One conclusion I have come to is that whatever the case may be, I'm going to always love my baby. She's innocent in all of this and with God's grace I will not allow this unusual circumstance of her birth to affect her upbringing.

I have a light breakfast of fruit and yogurt and settle down to wait on Mama. I only have an hour more till they get here.

I must have dozed off because I am woken up by voices entering the room.

"12 noon on the dot, talk about perfect timing eh!" Dad booms, as usual.

I smile at him as he walks over to kiss me. I don't think I could've loved any biological father more that this man right here. I give him a big hug in return while Mama stands in the middle of the room looking very uncomfortable.

"Where's Linc?" Dad asks.

"I don't know Dad. I tried to reach him all night, so did Woody but he didn't pick up his phone. I haven't heard from him this morning yet either."

"Hmm, I tried too. That man needs rapping to, maybe he'll show up while we're here. How's my grand-daughter doing?"

"Very well Dad, we'll all go see her shortly. By the way what happened to all your hair? And you've put on weight."

Dad has shaved his head bald; I can't even remember whether I've ever seen him looking like this before.

"It's my new look don't you like it? All the other young women seem to fancy me bald. Your mother has been quite concerned about it." he replies laughing.

Mama on the other hand makes a sort of grunting sound and sits down at the foot of my bed. That is the only sound she's made since she came in. I stare at her with raised eyebrows, willing her to get started. "Well Mama…" I prod.

"It's a long story Sydney but strangely it's also a short story. What brought this all up anyway?"

I pause, then launch into all the stunning information that Dr Rhodes had given us. I tell them about consanguinity and consanguineous relationships and the medical problems associated with them. I tell them about the statistics on 1st cousin marriages in the United States and Japan and worldwide. I inform them of the DNA test results done on Linc and I ending with the revelation that Linc according to those tests is my biological father!

I must have talked for at least fifteen minutes because by the time I finish I need to drink some water. Both Dad and Mama are silent. It seems everyone's reaction to the news is the same… silence! After a long pause Mama indicates she has something to say.

"What are the chances? Mercy me… *what* are the chances?" she repeats under her breath.

"You're going to have to speak louder than that dear, I know Sydney won't want to miss a word of what you're about to say." Dad interjects.

"Yes, I know. Sydney I'll start at the beginning but I think I should let you know first that I kept this from you all these years because I thought it was the best thing to do. I was sure I'd never need to tell you this. I love you and as any mother would do I'd protect you with all I've got … and even though the chance of this happening is statistically extremely rare, one in many millions I think I was told it seems to have happened to us!" She stops to catch her breath and then continues.

"About 3 or 4 years before you were born I had decided that I'd had enough of men. I'd had a couple of long term relationships that went sour and bitter breakups had followed. Coupled with my hectic studies, sports and business law ventures I felt I needed a break from emotional stress. I assumed I could go it alone when it came to parenting. Therefore I decided that since I didn't need or want a man in my life at the time, I would still go ahead and have a baby. That left me with several options. I could adopt or I could just find a man to get pregnant by and move on. I discarded both those options for various reasons. But I had another road I could travel down. This final option is what seems to have led us to where we are now. I've always believed that as a woman only *I* have the right to determine whether or not I want a child. And with today's technology it's possible to have one without having sex with some guy, just to achieve the same purpose. I researched getting pregnant via in-vitro fertilization using anonymous sperm from a sperm bank or cryobank as I think they are called nowadays. It took me over a year to decide if I was actually going to go through with it, all the while realizing that I could meet my dream guy at any time. I actually did meet my knight in shining armor....Jordan, but we met after you were born. You were two years old at the time. I must have spoken to and visited at least half a dozen sperm bank centers across the country before deciding on the particular one I used in Atlanta. I found out that I didn't even need to visit in person. I could have had the frozen sperm shipped to me anywhere in the world where invitro-fertilisation was conducted. As it turned out the process started with the center sending me about twenty individual profiles of men I would supposedly never meet. There were no names involved only numbers and alphabets to identify each profile. The profiles had consisted of height, weight, color of hair, color of eyes, whether African American or Asia or Caucasian. They also included what their careers were or if a student their GPAs and also their ages. I discovered through my research that over 70% of the sperm donors were men between the ages of nineteen and twenty-four, university students. Apparently they were all paid $50 each time they donated sperm. They often donated sperm very regularly, probably using the money they were being paid to offset their tuition, fees, books and pocket money! I also found out that each donor could have up to fifteen pregnancies against his identification numbers. Essentially it meant that any man, who has ever donated sperm under those circumstances at least at that particular center, could have up to fifteen kids scattered around the world somewhere."

Mama gets up from the foot of the bed and begins to pace up and down the room. I look over at Dad who for some reason doesn't meet my eyes. When she was ready Mama continues.

"I questioned the doctors, the medical staff and the management staff about the possibility of a meeting such as this. They told me it was next to impossible. How wrong they seem to have been proven! After I chose three or four possibles out of the initial profiles, I sent them back to the center. The process continued when they sent me back a more detailed set of facts on those three or four profiles. For example this more detailed information now included stuff like their blood type, medical history of themselves and even parents and grandparents. For instance whether or not anyone in his family had asthma or diabetes or if a close relative had died from stroke or heart failure. That type of stuff. Eventually I made my choice and lo and behold here you are!"

With that, Mama dramatically lifts up her hands. Very unlike her I hasten to add.

I hadn't known what to expect since last night when I'd last spoken to Mama but this certainly wasn't anywhere in my imagination. I don't know how to react, or what to say so I decide to ask a question.

"Is that all?"

"What do you mean is that all? Isn't that enough?"

Now I am angry!

"Don't get stroppy with me Mama. You took it upon yourself to put me through this. I didn't have a say or any choice in the matter did I? What made you think that any child of yours or any child in the world wouldn't want a father? I think it was a completely selfish decision. Luckily for me Dad has been the best dad anyone could possibly ever want. He loves me unconditionally; he's always been there for me come hell or high water. Why on earth would any woman think that a father isn't necessary? Oh and by the way, I don't agree with you that only women have a say in the birth of children!

If *I'd* been asked as a fetus I would have screamed out my answer…. *that I want a father to love, care, provide, tutor, protect and validate me, even to provide paternal discipline.* Millions of women across the globe especially in the western world complain bitterly about their men leaving them to fend for and care for their kids alone. Don't we all have names for such lackluster men? Deadbeat dads…isn't that the general term for such useless and uncaring fathers? Isn't that why they get thrown in jail when the courts and child support agencies catch up with them? Why Mama? Why would you intentionally set out to deprive me of such an important part of my life? Again I have to thank God for Dad. What would have happened if you hadn't met him? In other words I could have been one of those mal-aligned kids from a dysfunctional family background. Only in this case it wouldn't have been unforeseen circumstances that led to it, it would have been intentionally planned from the start! Oh but not to worry though, instead it seems I've ended up with a mal-aligned, dysfunctional marriage and as for *my* offspring…"

I have never spoken to my Ma in this tone before. Dad has his arm around me and is whispering for me to calm down, I realize I am shaking. I didn't know whether to disbelieve or accept everything Mama has just said. Of course I knew about invitro-fertilisation and cryobank centers but I never for the life of me thought *I* was a product of this kind of technology. But for all this to jell it means that Linc must have been a sperm donor while he was living in Atlanta. I know he graduated from Morehouse College in downtown Atlanta so maybe Mama's statistics were accurate. Maybe Linc had been one of those young men between the ages of nineteen and twenty-four that had donated a lot of sperm for money! Morally I know where I stand on that issue too. I can't figure out why these men didn't think of the millions of sperm they were offloading as potentially millions of children! I glance at over at Mama, she really is a piece of work, there's no sign of remorse or regret. She'd made her decision many years ago and come what may she's sticking with it.

"You were really selfish Mama." I continue.

"Obviously you were thinking only of yourself. Why don't you do the explaining to Teri when she's old enough? Yeh that's right, *you* tell her how you took it upon yourself to deprive a baby of a parent. On second thoughts no! I'll tell her myself. I'm not letting you near her ever again!

"Dad you hear me, I mean it." I rant.

"*If I had the power* I'd ban this arbitrary choice and practice that women like you take advantage of. I wish the technology were used only for women with prevailing medical conditions."

"Baby take it easy, maybe you'll be able to forgive your mother as time goes on. Okay?" Dad offers.

"Never in a million years! Dad have you known all of this for years? Or did you only just find out yourself?"

"I've known from within a few weeks of meeting your mother. She told me all those years ago. Biologically I could never have kids of my own so meeting you and Valerie was and has always been a double blessing."

"Did you agree with her not telling me Dad?"

"Actually no. Over the years, especially since you became a teenager we've argued over it many times. I have always believed you had a right to know but she'd sworn me to secrecy on the issue and so I had no choice but to keep my mouth shut. I'm sorry baby."

I could see Mama glaring at Dad angrily from over by the window. Her cell phone begins to ring; she excuses herself and walks out of the room.

"Dad…"

He hugs me again and we remain like that for a long while. I don't even realize that I am crying till Dad uses the corner of his crisp white handkerchief to wipe the tears away.

"Thanks Dad I love you."

"Let's go see Teri, baby, okay?"

"Alright Dad." I reply.

By the time we come back from seeing Teri, Mama, Ricky and Khreeo are waiting for us.

"Hey Sydney." says Ricky.

"We ran across Linc and Woody in the parking lot, they should be here any second. How's Teri?"

"She's great, thanks Ricky. What's up Khreeo?"

"It's all good girlfriend."

"Sydney honey, why don't you chew the fat with your friends for a while? Your mother and I will be back soon. I want to catch Linc in the lobby and speak to him." Dad prompts.

"No way Dad. As soon as Linc gets here Khreeo, Ricky and Woody will excuse us, right guys?"

"Of course Sydney, in fact Ricky and I will excuse you right now. We'll hurry Linc up when we see them."

"Thanks Khreeo. Just give us about 30 minutes please. Why don't you guys go see Teri anyway? You should talk to her Khreeo; just make sure Ricky doesn't try teaching her chess yet." I smile.

Ricky and Khreeo leave the room and a few seconds later Linc walks in. He walks over and gives Dad a big handshake and gives Mama a curt nod. He doesn't look much better than when I'd last seen him. This time however he has at least shaved. Dad is the first to speak. He goes on to relate to Linc everything Ma had disclosed about my birth and her reasons for it and even my reaction to it all. Throughout Dad's narrative Linc sits stony eyed and rigid. As soon as Dad concludes though, he had something to say.

"I've thought about it all night Sir and I've come to the conclusion that the only way this could have happened is just the way Valerie has said. As you know, I'm originally from Atlanta and I went to Morehouse. I do recall as a sophomore, donating sperm at one of those centers several times, possibly four or five times before I decided to stop. I haven't thought about that period more than twice in over twenty years. I remember being in between jobs and needing the money for books. This whole thing has knocked me for a loop and believe me when I say that I'm defeated, destroyed, disgusted. I really don't know how to handle this. My whole present and future has come crashing down. All I ever wanted since I left university was to have a loving, lovely wife and kids. When I married Sydney and then she got pregnant I thought all my dreams were coming true. Now this happens…"

All of a sudden Linc breaks down. He weeps, huge sobs racking his body. As a result I start crying again too. Woody, Ricky and Khreeo must have been just outside the door and had heard Linc weeping because they all came into the room together. It must have seemed like a disaster to them as they came in. Both Linc and I are weeping, Dad trying to calm both of us while Mama stares calmly out of the window. They all start speaking at the same time, causing further commotion till Lola also walks in and is able to quieten everyone.

We must have all stayed in my room for at least two hours. By the end of this time period the 'gang' has all learnt the full details. Dr. Hill and Dr. Rhodes had come and gone, adding further knowledge for us. Again it is Linc that first makes his excuses to leave. During the entire time he's been here he hasn't made any attempt to go see Teri. Ricky and Woody try to get him to stay longer but he refuses. By the time he did leave, minutes later, most of us present are both angry and very concerned about him.

"Does anyone know where Carla is?" asks Lola.

"I believe she can help us with Linc, she's always been particularly good at that sort of thing. We all know Ryoko is especially close to him but Carla has always been able to wield magic with Linc."

"Nobody seems to have spoken to her recently. I don't think she's on the road either 'cos she would have told one of us." Ricky mentions.

"You're right Ricky, I'll call her and if I don't get hold of her I'll call her agent. I met him a couple of times and I have his number." Woody offers.

Hours later we still haven't heard from Linc. We've been able to speak to Carla who is in New Jersey at a relative's place. She has promised to come back to New York immediately and help search for Linc.

Surprisingly Mama had left at 4p.m and gone about some business in the city. Dad and everybody else are still with me late into the evening when we get the call…

CHAPTER 35
LINCOLN CALDWELL

Friday January 30th
Brooklyn, NY

I usually only drink alcohol socially and even then in very small quantities. I've never been a real drinker like some of my buddies over the years. Today however I've drank a lot. A lot of vodka martinis to be exact, they had tasted pretty good too. I laugh out loud. I should have discovered this stuff much sooner. Why hadn't I joined in the drinking binges at college? Wow! If this is what the guys had experienced, I really had missed out.

Anyway back to reality…I can't take this anymore. Everything, my whole life has been destroyed. I want to call everyone I know and say something but I don't know what to say to them. Ah! I know who I'll call, she always knows what to say to me and vise versa.

"Hey Ryoko, pick up your damn phone…"

Why isn't she answering? Maybe she's playing 'hide the phone and go seek' like I am. I mean *I* haven't answered any of my calls all evening either. Ah hah here she is…

"Hello Linc is that you?" she asks.

"Yep it is."

"What's wrong? You sound funny are you drunk?"

"Drunk? Drunk is as drunk gets…oops! Sorry what did you say Ryoko?"

"Linc where are you? I got several calls from Woody and Ricky. They've told me all that's happened. Where are you? I'll come and meet you wherever. I'm sure things will turn out fine. Okay?"

"Brooklyn, I'm on Brooklyn Bridge. I'm trying to get a nice high vantage point so I can see the city lights better…"

"Brooklyn Bridge…, which end Linc?"

"I don't know. Don't worry about me. I just called to talk to you cutie."

"Linc, stay on the line I'm on my way."

I don't know what time it is. It's getting dark and the street lights are coming on. I can see some flashing blue and red and white lights in the distance. From where I am up here it doesn't really seem that far down. If only I could fly…

CHAPTER 36
SYDNEY COLLINS-CALDWELL

Friday January 30th
Manhattan, NY----continued

It Is Ryoko calling on Ricky's cell phone.

"Hey Ryoko what's cooking?" I hear him ask.

"Take it easy, take it easy. Where did you say he is?" he continues.

As I watch Ricky's countenance I see him lose color, it literally drains from his face. Even for a black man it is obvious. What on earth is she telling him? He turns and faces all of us, still listening to Ryoko on his phone.

"It's Linc. He's climbed up onto one of the pillions on Brooklyn Bridge; he's threatening to jump off! Ryoko also says he's intoxicated. She initially got a slurred call from him twenty minutes ago. She's already got a crew out at the scene, choppers and all. They are trying to coax him down. She also says he had stopped by her place very early this morning after driving aimlessly around the city all night. Apparently he'd been in pretty bad shape. She didn't know whether Sydney had seen him today yet. Well, I'm heading out. Who's coming with me?"

Long before he's finished speaking we are all hustling to get out of the room, including me.

"Where do you think you're going Sydney?" Lola asks.

"That's my husband out there." I shout back.

"I'm going out there even if I have to walk, understand me? No point trying to stop me, we're wasting time as it is let's go!" I shout again.

My heart is racing and thumping wildly in my chest. This has got to be the last wild twist in my story. I can hardly believe all this drama. As scared and as worried about Linc that I am, I still can't see him jumping off a bridge. Throughout the entire previous three weeks since the babies were born, he's been behaving strangely. We haven't even had a chance to sit and air our true feelings in their entirety. I don't even know for sure *what* Linc is feeling. Although it's obvious he's been distraught I never felt it was this bad. Do I know my husband that little? Am I such a bad judge of character?

Ricky is still speaking with Ryoko on his cell. I grab it from him.

"Is he alright Ryoko? Can you see him from where you are?"

"Yes I can Sydney but he's quite a way up. The helicopter lights are on him but he keeps threatening to let go while shielding his eyes from the beam. I'm worried that in his intoxicated state he could get too tired to hold on for much longer. The fall alone could be fatal not to mention Linc can't swim. How far away are you? I take it you're with Ricky and Khreeo."

"How far away are we Ricky?"

"Ten more minutes." He replies.

Ryoko is telling me that Linc can hear her through the police megaphone she is using *but he can't hear her, or can he?* She says there's too much background noise and he'd dropped his cell phone a while ago. It had fallen into the river below. Traffic of course is at a standstill and a large crowd has already gathered at the scene. We are going to find it a little difficult getting close enough to talk to him but Ryoko has arranged police escort as soon as we were in sight. I pray under my breath…Father God have mercy on me and spare my husband and daughter…

Screams! I could hear screams and louder voices.

"What's happening Ryoko, What's going on?" I manage to splutter into the phone.

"He's fallen or jumped, we're not sure which. He's hit the water and gone under. The police divers are already in the water too. They jumped into the river from the police boats that had been called to patrol under the bridge. We'll find him Sydney don't worry too much. There isn't too much of a freeze on the river tonight so he wouldn't have hit solid ice. I saw him go straight down and I saw the splash. We'll get him."

"Faster Ricky, you've got to go faster Linc has fallen or jumped the police aren't sure which but he's in the freezing water…hurry."

All I can do now is sit impatiently as Ricky drives as quickly and recklessly as possible to the scene.
I continued to pray…O God…

EPILOGUE
SYDNEY COLLINS-CALDWELL

Sunday February 22nd
Boston, MA

Am I a widow? Or am I not?

They say hindsight is 20:20 and experience can be a harsh teacher. It's been three weeks and two days since Linc had gone missing. The police had dragged the river for days and days but his body has still not been found. I'm trying to get on with my life but it's proving extremely difficult without full closure on Linc, like I have with Teri's sister. What I really want to do is leave the country, maybe go to Europe. Spain or England to be exact, a change of scenery is what I'm recommending for Teri and myself. She has come through her treatment of chemotherapy with flying colors and doesn't even need the BMT, at least not yet.

With the level of despondency and dejection that Linc had shown prior to his fall from the Brooklyn Bridge, he should have been hospitalized for clinical depression. I recently found out that new medical experiments have shown that it may be possible to detect and therefore prevent people from attempting suicide, something to do with the detection of excessive levels of cortisol secreted in a person's body when undergoing extreme stress. I have now come home to familiar Boston, my home away from home and I've found a small level of solace. Dad has been brilliant but Mama…what can I say? My goal now is to live life and live it blessed and abundantly. I still pray that Linc's body be found but even more so I pray for a miracle…that he is found alive and well. I look up at the beautiful clear blue sky and at the few white birds swooping back and forth and I remember…My God is a miracle working God and He is the same yesterday, today and forevermore. The miracles He performed in ages past He still performs to this day. All I need is faith…………Amen!

About the Author
Toyin Adon-Abel

Toyin Adon-Abel is both a former British Police Officer and former British Prison Warden. He is a British citizen and currently resides in the United States of America as a permanent resident.

The subject matter of A Woman's Secret...sperm donation & consanguineous relationships; are issues that modern society is seemingly unaware of all the potential pitfalls. Toyin raises the question, are all scientific and technological advances morally acceptable?

Toyin feels that women do have the right to choose how and when to give birth. However he also feels that both men and society in general have to be fully aware of the possible negative consequences, as well as the immediately foreseeable future.

Look out for the first sequel that continues the saga of 3 generations of the Collins and Caldwell families: 'A Woman's Rage.'

Lightning Source UK Ltd.
Milton Keynes UK
03 January 2011

165120UK00001B/17/P